A Little Girl's Story

A Collection of Short Stories

Tristen Synclair

ISBN: 9798991544603

For all the beautiful people
who helped this little girl
find her way

Preface

This collection of stories is, as a whole, a fictional representation of my growing up. Printed in chronological order of when I began writing, the first story dates back to when I was eight years old while the last was finished my first week out of the house. Some of the stories grew with me to take on greater meanings while others have hardly been altered from their original form. From the cheesy princess dreams of my childhood to the allegories born from heartbreak, I hope these snapshots in time will make you laugh and pique your intellect. Above all, however, I hope you find something that outlasts the printed word.

-Tristen Synclair

Table of Contents

Princess Fiona

In a magical land, there lived a beautiful princess. She was so beautiful she looked like an angel, and the people of the kingdom were constantly saying she was the prettiest girl they had ever laid eyes on.

Her name was Fiona and she loved flowers. The young princess had a whole field of flowers, but they weren't ordinary flowers.

When Fiona was five, her father and mother gave her a flower that could grant one wish. Do you know what Fiona wished for? She wished that there was a whole field of them. That's how her magical meadow was created.

When Fiona was 10, she and her three friends—Peter, John, and Smith—were playing in the meadow. Now, since they were kids, they couldn't resist wishing for something.

Peter picked one of the flowers and whispered to it, "I wish I were a knight." In an instant, he was tall and clothed in shiny, silver armor.

Fiona picked up a flower and—glancing over at Peter—whispered, "I wish I was a princess locked in a tower with John and Smith." In a flash, a tall tower popped out of the meadow with Fiona, John, and Smith in it.

Peter stared up at the tall tower. "Uh oh," he said. He hadn't been planning on having to rescue his friends from an extremely tall tower. Peter was brave and funny but, in the end, he got his friends down.

Six years later, Fiona's mother and father were hosting a party to celebrate Fiona's birthday. All the men from the neighboring kingdoms had been invited because the king and queen believed it was high time their daughter should marry.

Fiona fell in love with Edward, and the next day her mother took the two to Honeymoon Park.

"Fiona," the queen said, "when I married your father, a fairy came to me and told me, 'When your firstborn daughter falls in love, she must get married the next day.' I was never told the reason, but I am going to obey anyway. When we return to the palace, your wedding will take place."

Just as Fiona's mother said, she and Edward were married when they returned to the palace. Of course, they lived happily ever after.

A Little Girl's Story

Once upon a time, there lived a little girl. She lived in a happy little meadow, in a faraway land, long ago. In this meadow, the days are endless and there is no divide between the heavens and the earth, so the little girl played with animals and sun rays alike, friends who understood her and cared for her.

Of them all, however, she was the fondest of one particular ray of sun, and it was fond of her. It would tell her stories, shine on her as she twirled on the swing tied to the elm tree, and decorate her hair with the finest roses in the meadow. It cared for her as no one else did, and the little girl was happy.

One day the little girl was walking along the border of the meadow when a little bird landed on a nearby tree. "Good morning!" It greeted.

"Good morning!" The little girl replied. "How's everything going?"

"Wonderful!" The bird sang. "Just wonderful, but it's not the present that should be questioned."

"What do you mean?" The little girl asked, a shadow of concern coming across her face. Foreboding was an unknown feeling in the meadow.

"Strange seasons are coming," the little bird replied. "I can feel it, tiny shifts in the temperature and wind. The sun is going to go away."

For one horrific, pain-drenched moment, the little girl became deaf to the entire world. All she could hear was a singular thought: *No. NO!!!!*

If the sun went away, she would never get the chance to tell her ray how much she loved it, which meant that her ray of sun would never know how much she cared. This thought broke the little girl's heart.

Sleep eased her ache, but as the first dawn spilled over a suddenly apparent horizon, the little girl's usual smile faded. Why had it been dark? What was darkness? Fear crept into her heart as she took in her surroundings. She was no longer in the meadow she loved so dearly but trapped in a cave nestled in a bordering mountain range.

In a panic, the little girl ran to the boulder blocking the cave's entrance. Through small openings between the stone and the cave wall, the little girl could see her friends and her beloved ray of sun. They were leaving the meadow, which was descending into darkness.

The little girl tried calling out to them, but they had already traveled out of earshot. She pushed and pulled on the stone, but it would not budge. She turned to the back of the cave where fleeting light graced tunnel entrances of all shapes and sizes. She could try exploring for another exit, but there was no guarantee she would come across one and it was highly possible to get hopelessly lost.

With the last rays of sunlight slipping her into utter darkness, the little girl sank to a seat on the cold stone floor.

Like the water slowly dripping from the cave ceiling, tears began to roll down her cheeks as she realized the unlikelihood of ever again resting under the sun's warm rays. Never again would she laugh along or play with her wonderful friends. Never again would it be possible for her to wear a smile on her heart.

With these thoughts in her mind, the little girl's tears turned into a stream that flowed ceaselessly until the sound of snickering caused her to come to a sniffling halt.

The little girl looked around until she could just make out two bats hanging from the ceiling of the cave. They had once been two of her friends in the meadow, so they knew about her relationship with her ray of sun.

In hopes of receiving some comfort from them, the little girl tried to tell them of the pain she was feeling, but they only mocked her saying, "Oh! Where's your prince to save you, princess?"

The little girl concluded that they had never known true happiness and, when they met someone who had, they would try to make it as miserable as them. So the little girl listened to what they had to say and then walked away, a tear rolling down her cheek as she thought, *They don't understand. No one understands.*

So alone the little girl sat—for days that turned into weeks that turned into months—releasing a seemingly endless stream of tears, until one night when rays of light illuminated the boulder that blocked the cave's opening.

It was the moon.

The little girl was so shocked to see light that she did not know what to do at first. Then, after a while, she began to feel happy. Although the moon's rays were not enough to warm her, they gave the little girl hope, and hope was what she had been wanting for a long time.

The little girl became very fond of the moon. She found it curious how they were separated by a wall of stone yet the moon stayed in front of the cave to talk to her. It would tell her about its life and the little girl would happily listen, sometimes sharing something about hers. It felt so wonderful to have a friend again, but her joy was blinding her.

The little girl, with happiness in her heart, fell under the presupposition that the moon would stay forever. She forgot that her cave-dwelling prevented any sustainment of light so, before she knew what was happening, or could even say goodbye, dark clouds suddenly covered her beloved friend.

The little girl spent a lot of time thereafter at the cracks around the big stone looking for the moon. Sometimes she would see it but, when the moon saw her, it would hide behind the dark clouds.

The more she watched for the moon, the more depressed she became because she saw that it was growing up. It was growing up without her and it seemed to be just fine. This broke the little girl's heart because the moon was doing fine and she was not. She was angry, sad, and broken all at once. She wanted to cry, but the tears would not come.

As much as she would have loved to be with the moon again, the little girl decided that — if someone told her they could bring her friend back — she would turn them down. She did not know exactly why she decided this, she just thought it was better this way. So, once again, the little girl sat alone in her cave, for not even the two bats bothered her anymore.

Then one clear, cloudless night, a very mean, outraged, and wounded firefly entered the cave and fell at the little girl's feet. Surprised, she picked the poor thing up and began nursing it back to health.

Although the firefly often got angry at her, the little girl did not fight back. She had been through enough pain to recognize it and therefore knew that fighting would only make it worse. But it wasn't just that. The little girl saw something in that firefly, something that had become quite rare in her life: light.

So the little girl took care of the firefly. She encouraged it and showed it how to be nice. The firefly was not the most eager student, but the little girl was patient and, as every day passed, the firefly became nicer and its light grew brighter.

As the years passed, the little girl became quite fond of the firefly and, deep inside, had a feeling that this small, weak source of light was hope for a companion-filled future.

One day the little girl was walking around her cave, thinking about the life she once lived in the meadow. The little girl had not told the firefly about her past, so the firefly was confused about why she was walking away from it. Not knowing what else to do, it followed.

The firefly kept asking her why she was walking away, but the little girl was in too much pain to answer. The firefly began throwing small rocks at her, but she still would not answer.

The firefly only had one category for such behavior so, after a long time of repeating this process, it came up next to her and asked, "For the one-hundredth time, why are you angry?"

The little girl, slightly annoyed, replied, "For the one-hundredth time, I'm not angry."

The firefly walked to the stone blocking the cave's entrance. It stopped, turned its head, said, "I thought you were nice," and then left the cave through a crack.

The little girl, whose back had been to the firefly, turned her head and sadly whispered, "I thought you cared."

She watched the firefly drift away, heartbroken that it never looked back. To her surprise, tears suddenly appeared in the corners of her eyes. Puzzled by their sudden appearance after lengths of absence and broken by the firefly's departure, the little girl slid to the ground where sobs shook her body.

I thought this one was different, she thought, head buried in her knees. *It was doing so well, it grew so much, and it changed for the better. Why did it leave, too?*

After a while, the little girl began to pull herself back together. With the vanishment of each source of light, it was becoming easier to acclimate to darkness and loneliness. Experience aided this capability, but also the revelation that she never had harbored genuine love for those she had exalted. Whatever fancy she might have felt simply came from her innate desire to be loved. She had no true connection with the ray of sun. Thus, after much wasted affection, she was finally able to move on.

One spring afternoon, the little girl stood by the cave's barricaded entrance enjoying the pleasant breeze that slipped past. Even though she had been battling with a sense of meaninglessness and feeling loneliness like a knife to the heart, today she breathed in the new life the season brought.

This is where the little boy found her.

He came from the tunnels she reasoned herself out of exploring. Trapped like her yet looking around, he found her in the chamber she had been living in, and the torch that lit his way illuminated every nook and cranny.

The little girl was very curious about the little boy. He was unlike anyone she had met before. Yet, knowing her track record, the little girl refused to become attached to her new friend.

This is just another silly fancy that will soon be over, she resolved. Yet, their friendship continued until one day the little girl sighed and acknowledged the sentiments blooming in her heart.

She found a home in the little boy, a safe place where she was comfortable and could let her guard down. Someone she could talk with like she did with herself, yet the two didn't need words to understand each other. They could just *be* with each other, as if silence is something one can be fluent in. He became her best friend and they understood each other as if they shared souls.

He was the skepticism to her trustfulness and she was the imagination to his realism. He was the logic to her emotion, she the voice of his perplexion, and he the calm to her storm. They fit together like pieces in a puzzle.

As the two grew closer, the little girl was frightened to find herself the harbor of an affection significantly stronger than any she had felt before. She wanted to care for the little boy, not for what she might gain in return but because of what she could give.

And then the little boy left.

They had to part, that's all he would say. She did not understand the idea and her very nerves screamed out in rebellion, but she knew she could trust him.

If he believed leaving to be the right decision, she would let him go. And he did, so she did, but every step he took into the gnarly twists of tunnels at the back of the cave caused reality to sink deeper in the little girl's heart.

She was losing her best friend.

She had lost before, things she idolized, childhood fancies, bonds that only existed in her head. They were nothing compared to what she and the little boy came to have, but losing them broke her.

She had recovered, but here she was: losing something real, allowing one of the best things that had ever happened to her to walk away. Things had walked away before, but this time she could choose differently.

Was she really going to let this happen?

Was she really going to let herself lose him?
Was she going to blindly trust him?
Or was she going to fight for what was theirs?

Everything in her wanted to run after the little boy, but separation was what he wanted and she loved him enough to grant him his wish, no matter the cost to herself.

The darkness that followed was deeper than any she had seen before.

Yet, at this bitter end, the little girl realized—like every time before—she was still able to make out her surroundings. While there was no tangible source, there was a distinct essence illuminating her surroundings: *the* Light.

With what she held dear suddenly absent from her life, the little girl had no choice but to rely on the Light to make her way around the enveloping darkness. It was in this swing of maintaining sanity and feeling coherent that the little girl found her identity not in what she had lost but in what she had always had.

Like a lock tried by every key on the chain but one, this shift clicked in the most counterintuitive way so the girl—who was not so little anymore—found something to rejoice about in the cave where she had seen so much darkness.

It was here, where she could barely make out her surroundings, that she was the most aware of the Source that had been sustaining her all along.

The girl closed her eyes and smiled. She wasn't alone. She had never been alone.

The inside of her eyelids suddenly became so bright the girl interrupted her thoughts to look around. Shielding her eyes, the girl made her way forward to find herself standing in the previously blocked entrance of the cave, the meadow stretching out before her.

The girl took a step. It was so bright, so beautiful, soft, golden, and lovely. She saw those she had long since been separated from prancing about and laughing giddily. She could join them if she wished, step into their blissful ignorance and forget everything she had experienced.

The girl took another step. It was all there, just out of reach, the happiness she had so longed for. She just had to take it. The only thing holding her back was herself.

Herself. That's what she had gained over the years. She had come so far from the little girl who woke up in the cave. She had come to know herself and Who sustained her. Yes, she had lost more than she could ever give, but through the loss, she had gained more than she could ever find.

She could latch on to her newfound freedom and forever run like a leaf in a breeze, but to forget everything she had learned, the girl reckoned, was not worth the trade.

Spotting a small boulder just beyond where she had been blocked in, the girl lowered herself to a seat. She would stay.

The meadow may have had everything she ever wanted,
but sitting there in the cave's entrance, aware of *the* Light's
presence, she had everything she could need.

Lauren's Royal Life

"That is such a beautiful dress!" Lauren exclaimed. She and her three friends, Cathy, Emma, and Katie, were spending their Saturday afternoon doing their favorite thing: shopping.

"I agree," Katie said. "It is the most beautiful gown I've ever seen."

"Too bad," Emma said. "Look at the price tag. It costs a fortune!"

"Oh my!" Cathy exclaimed, staring at the price tag.

"Well," Lauren said with a sigh, "we might as well keep looking. Maybe the shop down the street is more affordable. Come on, girls."

"Wait," Emma said. "Do you hear that?"

"What is it?" Katie asked.

"It sounds like hoofbeats," Emma replied. "I think a horse is coming our way."

"Do you think it's the royal page?" Lauren asked, suddenly excited.

"Oh, I do hope so!" Cathy exclaimed. "Maybe he'll have grand news, like an invitation to a ball at the palace!"

"Calm down, Cathy," Emma soothed.

"Here it comes!" Lauren exclaimed as a horse galloped into the town circle. "It *is* the royal page!"

A loud trumpet sounded, and the royal page pulled out a piece of paper and began to read, "His Majesty, King James II, who misses his daughter very much, has decided to adopt another daughter from the common folk. His royalty will pick one with the qualities of a princess to replace his daughter, who has married and gone to live with her prince in his kingdom. Come dressed in your finest clothes and be at the palace at noon in two days' time. Signed, King James II."

With his message relayed, the royal page left as quickly as he had come.

Lauren and her friends looked at each other. They were all daughters of the common folk. There was one moment of silence as they made that connection, then the next, they—and every one of their surrounding peers—became giddy with frantic excitement. A chance to become royalty?! This was the opportunity of a lifetime!

"Well, come on!" Cathy exclaimed. "Let's go find some gowns!" And the four of them made hasty progress to the next shop in their path.

Lauren imagined what it would be like to be a princess, but she didn't think anyone would pick her. She was only a poor blacksmith's daughter, not royalty. Regardless, she had to look her best.

Two days went by faster than Lauren thought they would, but she was ready. An hour 'till noon, she and her three best friends headed off to the palace.

"It's— It's— It is.....beyond description," Katie said, staring up at the spires and turrets of the palace as they passed through the main gate.

Hundreds and hundreds of other girls were doing the same, excitedly whispering amongst themselves as palace guards directed them into the central courtyard. There they would wait to be inspected by the king.

Tension was high as the hours began to slowly pass. Maiden after maiden, girl after girl, walked out of the palace gates and back home.

When their turn came, Emma went in and was rejected. Cathy went in and was turned down. Katie went in and was escorted out with an "I'm sorry." But they all hung around to wait for Lauren.

"This way, Madame," a palace guard directed.

"Good luck," Katie said.

"It's gonna be fine," Cathy said.

"Just go in there and give them your best," Emma said.

So Lauren took a deep breath and followed the guard into the royal palace.

As they walked through hall after hall, Lauren stared in awe at all the finery that hung on the walls or lay on a table. There were tapestries of every kind, vases of gold, wonderful flowers, and rugs from all over the world. Lauren had never seen so many riches in her life. When they finally stopped in what was obviously the throne room, Lauren saw the king and almost didn't shake her wonder in time to bow.

"Good day, young mistress," he greeted. "And what might your name be?"

"Lauren," she replied, suddenly very nervous. "Lauren Louise Lanford, your grace."

The king asked Lauren all sorts of questions. Basic questions like where she was born, how old she was, who her parents were, and where she lived. But also questions like, "What would you do if you were strolling through town and someone bumped into an old maid, scattering her belongings all over the street?"

To Lauren, it was not a very hard question. "I would rush over," she immediately replied, "help her gather them up, and then escort her home."

One hour passed, and Lauren began to feel comfortable around the king. But she was still a little nervous about whether he would pick her as the new princess.

It happened to turn out that the king loved Lauren and saw all the right qualities of a princess in her. So he led her to his balcony and declared to everyone remaining in the courtyard, "I have found my new daughter!"

Everyone was very quiet. Most of the maidens were very unhappy, but three—Cathy, Emma, and Katie—were overjoyed for their friend.

"I now declare," continued the king, "That from this moment on Lauren Louise Lanford shall be known as Princess Lauren!" Then the king turned to Lauren and placed an intricate diamond tiara on her head.

Trumpets sounded and the guards began to usher the other maidens out of the courtyard as Lauren was brought back to the throne room.

The king then called the royal page and said, "Send a letter to Lauren's parents saying, 'To the parents of Lauren Louise Lanford, I write to tell you that your daughter has been picked as the new princess. I would like you to pack up her belongings and send them to the castle. You are allowed to visit her anytime you like but must remember that she belongs to me now. Signed, King James II.'"

The royal page finished writing and then left to deliver the news.

Next, the king called a maid and said to her, "Julia, escort Princess Lauren to her sleeping chambers."

Lauren bid the king goodnight and then followed the maid named Julia.

Lauren's room was unlike anything she'd seen before. The ceilings stretched far above her head and jewels decorated everything from the corners of the bed frame to the ornate dresser.

Lauren cautiously made her way inside while Julia made sure everything was set for the night. Satisfied, she said goodnight to Lauren and left her to sleep.

Lauren went to the large picture window and opened it. She could see a lot of the kingdom from this vantage point. A soft evening breeze blew over her and Lauren took a deep breath. There would be a lot to learn tomorrow, so Lauren closed the window and went to bed.

The next morning, Lauren awoke to find Julia opening Lauren's new wardrobe. Inside, Lauren was shocked to find all the costly dresses she had seen hanging before her in the shop the other day.

"What would you like to wear today, Princess Lauren?" Julia asked.

"Oh. I don't know," Lauren said. "You pick."

"Oh, I couldn't, Princess," Julia replied. "I'm only a maid."

"Please, I insist," Lauren said.

"Yes, Princess," Julia answered.

"And please," Lauren encouraged, "call me Lauren."

"Yes, Princ— Lauren."

Julia picked out a dress and helped Lauren into it. Then she led the new princess to breakfast.

Lauren found it difficult to walk in a dress made of so many layers of fabric, but she managed to make it to the great hall without tripping.

As Julia directed, Lauren sat down in the seat left of the king, and Julia left to attend to her other duties.

"If I may ask, your grace," Lauren said to the king.

"Of course," the king replied. "Ask anything you like."

"Where is Queen Elizabeth?" Lauren asked. "I have heard many stories about her, unless they were all tall tales and there is no Queen."

"Oh no, there is a queen," said King James. "She has been on a secret vacation for a couple of days and will be back around our midday meal."

"Does she know I am here?" Lauren asked, getting a little worried.

"Yes," the king said. "She knew that I would be choosing a new daughter. She also knew that there would be millions of girls at the palace the day I chose. You see, the queen does not like big crowds or lots of attention, so she went on a private vacation until after the selection."

"Oh," Lauren said, as breakfast was brought in.

They ate in silence as Lauren stared in wonder at the food. There was bacon, eggs, sausage, pancakes, waffles, orange juice, water, and milk. Lauren had never seen such a fine meal in her life.

Once Lauren and the king were full, with a lot left over, Lauren asked if she could leave the table.

"Of course," said the king with a smile.

So Lauren set out to explore the palace, hoping that she would not get lost.

Lauren went back to her room, and then from there made it back to the throne room, and from there she somehow remembered her way back to the courtyard.

As she stepped outside, a lovely fall breeze was there to welcome her, and so was a girl and a horse.

Lauren walked over and said, "Hello."

The girl jumped and turned around. When she saw who was behind her, she gasped and curtsied.

"Your Highness," she said and then rose.

"It's a pleasure to meet you, too, and call me Lauren. What is your name?"

"My name is Rachel," the girl answered.

"What is your job, Rachel?" Lauren asked.

"My job is to train horses," Rachel answered. "Whenever a new or wild horse is bought or captured by the king or his guards, I ride the horse and get it used to its new gear."

"Very interesting," Lauren said. "Well, I'm going to go explore some more. It was nice talking to you."

"You too, Lauren," Rachel replied.

With that, they went their separate ways.

Lauren looked around the courtyard and then decided to go left, again hoping she'd be able to find her way back. She explored the extensive royal gardens and eventually arrived at what seemed to be the royal stables. There she found a girl feeding a horse and its colt, so Lauren walked over to her.

"Hello," Lauren said, and the girl jumped in surprise like Rachel had. "What is your name?" Lauren asked.

The girl replied, "My name is Felicity, Princess."

"Please, call me Lauren."

"As you wish," the girl replied.

"What do you do, Felicity?" Lauren asked.

"I take care of the horses," Felicity answered. "I feed them, groom them, and mend their wounds. Of course, I don't do it all alone, other maids help me. There are way too many horses for one to care for by herself at the palace."

Lauren's tummy growled. "Pardon me," she said, "exploring the palace grounds must have used up my food supply."

"Oh, it's okay, Lauren," said Felicity, pulling out her pocket watch. "It is time for lunch anyway. Would you like me to lead you to the dining hall?"

"That's okay," Lauren said. "I think I can find my way back. Thank you for the offer, though."

"You're welcome," Felicity replied.

Lauren tried to remember her way back and luckily made it without issue.

Just as she sat down where she had for breakfast, lunch was brought in.

Again the meal was too great to eat it all, and Lauren wondered how she would ever get used to such meals.

After lunch, Lauren began to explore the inside of the palace. Soon after she had begun, the sound of trumpets drew her back to the courtyard.

When she arrived at the front steps of the palace, she saw a beautiful carriage that must have just arrived.

The trumpets blew again, a guard opened the carriage door, and a lovely lady stepped out. She was so lovely Lauren knew at once that she was the queen.

Her head was adorned with light brown hair, green eyes, and pink lips. She was wearing a gorgeous red dress with strips of gold down the middle.

"Hello," the queen said. "I am Queen Elizabeth, and you must be the new princess."

Lauren nodded. Meeting the king was one thing, but the queen— way more intense.

"What is your name?" The queen asked.

"Lauren," said Lauren, and then her heart skipped a beat. "Oh!" Lauren quickly shook away her awe and curtsied.

How on earth could I forget to curtsy to the queen herself!? Lauren thought. *Being a princess has really gone to your head, Lauren! Don't you ever forget to curtsy to the queen again! It's a good thing she is nice, otherwise she would have you beheaded.*

"I am so sorry, your grace," Lauren said. "I was just shocked, I didn't mean to be rude."

"That's all right," the queen said. "I was just beginning to wonder if my husband had made the wrong decision. Would you like a tour of the castle?"

"I would be honored, your majesty," Lauren replied.

The queen smiled, "You can call me, mother."

"Of course, your majes— I mean, mother." And with that, they started their tour.

The queen showed Lauren every nook and cranny of the palace. She showed Lauren the ballroom, the tearoom, the kitchen, the bedrooms, the dining hall, the lookout post, the dungeon, and lastly the letter room.

Thinking of letters reminded Lauren of Cathy, Emma, and Katie. "I have three best friends back in the village," Lauren told the queen. "I was wondering if you would mind if I invited them to tea."

"I would not mind at all," the queen replied. "We can have it in two days."

"Oh, thank you very much!" Lauren exclaimed.

Queen Elizabeth went back to the throne room while Lauren began to write her letter.

Lauren happily sealed the letter in an envelope and called the royal page.

The next day, the castle was in a bustle. All of the maids were cooking, cleaning, and decorating. Within all of this, Lauren made a new friend. Her name was Chrissa. Chrissa's job at the palace was to mend old clothes and make new ones.

Lauren really liked Chrissa and discovered that they had a lot of things in common. They talked all day as Chrissa sewed, and Lauren was surprised when Julia came in saying that it was time to go to bed.

While Lauren was getting ready for bed, she remembered that tomorrow was the royal tea party!

Lauren awoke early and got dressed. Then she went to the dining hall to check if everything was ready.

The tea was boiling, treats were on the table, and everything was decorated. *Just right,* Lauren thought, and then her mind wandered back to the merry conversation she had with Chrissa the day before.

I wonder, Lauren thought. *Maybe Queen Elizabeth will let Chrissa come to the tea party, too. I'm sure Cathy, Emma, and Katie will enjoy her as much as I did.* Lauren went to the throne room to ask.

"Of course she can come," the queen said. "I believe she would enjoy a break."

"Thank you very much!" Lauren replied.

"You're welcome," the queen said, as Lauren left to tell Chrissa.

Chrissa was not so easily convinced.

"Oh Lauren," she said, "I would love to go, but—"

"But what?" Lauren asked.

"I have a lot of sewing to do," Chrissa answered.

"But Queen Elizabeth said you could go," Lauren replied.

Chrissa, still unsure, answered, "All right, I'll go."

"Okay," Lauren said. "You're going to need a dress—"

"Check!" Chrissa interrupted.

"A hair ribbon—"

"Check!"

"Along with makeup."

"Uh, Lauren…?" Chrissa said.

"Yes?"

"I don't have makeup!"

Lauren thought for a moment, "Well…..um, you can use mine!"

"Okay!" Chrissa said.

When Chrissa was finished dressing, they chatted a little, and then Julia knocked on the door.

"Come in," Lauren said.

"Princess Lauren," Julia said, "your guests have arrived."

Lauren and Chrissa smiled. As they left the room, Lauren said to Julia, "Remember, call me Lauren."

"I will," Julia said. "It just takes a little getting used to."

Lauren smiled, and she and Chrissa hurried downstairs to welcome the three guests.

"Hi, Cathy! Hi, Emma! Hi, Katie! Welcome to the castle!" Lauren said all excited. "This is Chrissa, she is one of the maids. Her job here is to mend old clothes and to make new ones. The queen said she could come to the tea party. I thought you would like to meet her."

"Um, Lauren?" Emma asked. "Did we come here for a talk or a tea party?"

"Both!" Lauren exclaimed.

They all laughed, as Lauren led them to the tea room.

"Mmmm!" Katie said as she bit into one of the scones. "These are delicious!"

"Thank you," Lauren answered. "Julia and the other cooks are very talented."

"Well then remind me to hire them for my next birthday party!" Cathy joked, and everyone laughed.

After tea, Lauren led everyone outside. The first thing that caught Chrissa's eye was one of the royal gardens in the distance.

"Oh, Lauren, can we go to that garden?" Chrissa asked. "I've always been so busy inside sewing that I never had a chance to explore them."

"Of course we can!" Lauren answered.

A few minutes later, when they arrived at the garden, Lauren exclaimed, "Hello, Iris!"

"Hello, Lauren!" Iris replied. "It's nice to see a lovely princess on a lovely day. I see you brought some friends with you."

"Yes, Iris," Lauren said. "These are my friends Cathy, Emma, and Katie. I'm pretty sure you know Chrissa."

"Yes, I do," Iris answered.

"Iris, why do you like flowers?" Cathy asked.

"Because they are so pretty," Iris replied.

"I could have guessed that!" Cathy said. "Everyone loves flowers because they are so beautiful."

"I agree," Emma said. "The flowers you have here at the palace are the prettiest I have ever seen."

Katie, who was getting a little bored with flowers, asked, "Are there any horses here? I love horses."

"Yes, of course," Lauren answered. "Follow me."

They said goodbye to Iris and followed Lauren to the stables.

When they arrived, Rachel was standing outside.

"Hello, Princess Lauren," she said, then caught herself. "Forgive me. Hello, Lauren. Are these the friends you invited to this tea party I've been hearing so much about?"

"Yes," Lauren replied. "These are my three best friends from the village and Chrissa."

"Well it's nice to meet you all," Rachel said. "Lauren, would you like to take your horse Lucy for a ride?"

"Yes!" Lauren replied. "I would enjoy that very much. Do you mind if we get other horses so all of us can ride?"

"Of course!" Rachel said. "What a brilliant idea!"

"Just to be safe," Lauren said. "Does everyone here know how to ride a horse?"

It turned out Katie and Emma were the only ones who weren't exactly sure how.

"That's all right!" Rachel said. "We can do some sharing. Lauren, you'll ride Lucy, and we can decide who wants to ride on Prince, Beauty, and Heidi." Rachel then went into the stables and shortly returned with three beautiful horses in tow.

"Oh!" Katie exclaimed. "I want to ride this one!" She ran over to the brown horse with white spots.

"That is Heidi," Rachel said.

"Heidi," Katie whispered. "That is such a pretty name. Will you ride her with me?"

"Of course," Rachel said, smiling softly at Katie. She turned back to the other girls and saw Emma and Chrissa hopping onto Beauty while Cathy mounted Prince.

"Okay then," Lauren said. "Let's ride!"

The horses turned the corner, and they left the stables.

A while into their ride, the girls were galloping around a corner when all of a sudden Katie screamed. Everyone looked back at her.

"Look!" Katie exclaimed, pointing toward the front of their assembly. Everyone looked forward and then jerked the horses to a stop.

"Willow!" Rachel exclaimed. "What do you think you're doing standing in the middle of the road!?"

Willow looked at them with a guilty expression. "I'm sorry," she said. "I was training my chipmunks how to cross the road."

"What chipmunks?" Lauren asked. She didn't see any around.

"These," Willow said, looking behind her. "Come on, guys. It's all right. Everything's safe now."

Hearing these words, two little chipmunks peeped out from behind her.

"Aww!" Katie gushed. "They're so cute!"

Everyone then got off their horses and played with the little baby chipmunks.

All too soon, it was evening, and Lauren and her friends had to part.

"Thanks for the tea party," Emma said.

"Yes," Cathy said. "It was loads of fun."

"I loved the horses," Katie said. "And you did a lovely job giving us a tour of the castle."

"We will have to do it again sometime," Lauren said as her three friends stepped into the carriage that was to take them home.

"Goodbye," Katie said, as she stepped in.

Lauren walked over to the window and said, "It shan't be a goodbye."

Then she stepped back and smiled at her friends before turning to the driver and saying, "Take them home."

As she watched the carriage drive away, a gust of cold wind blew. *Burr,* Lauren shivered. She knew winter was almost there.

While Lauren was getting ready for bed, she noticed winter clothes in her wardrobe. They looked so toasty and warm, and she couldn't wait to wear them.

The next morning, Lauren got dressed, brushed her hair, and then went downstairs for breakfast.

After a hearty breakfast with the king and queen, Lauren went back up to her room.

When she walked in, Lauren saw a girl. "You must be Dianna," Lauren said.

"Yes, I am," the girl replied.

"Queen Elizabeth told me just now at breakfast that her sister's daughter would be staying with us now. She is going to have a ball this evening to celebrate you as our royal guest."

"Oh, I can't wait!" Dianna said.

That evening, Lauren and Dianna went up to their room to get dressed. They were so excited.

Everyone in the kingdom was invited, and the two girls knew that they had to look their best.

"What to wear, what to wear," Lauren said as she and Dianna dug through all the clothes in their wardrobes.

"Oh!" Dianna exclaimed as she pulled out a pink dress. "Look at this gown, Lauren! Isn't it lovely!"

"It is," Lauren said, eying the outfit. "But look at this one." She pulled out a glorious gold dress.

"My, my," Dianna said. "That dress is lovely too. Is this what we're going to wear?"

"Yes," Lauren said. "The answer is so yes."

They giggled and began to help each other get dressed.

What seemed like hours later, Julia came up and told the two girls that the party had begun.

Lauren and Dianna entered the ballroom, where there seemed to be millions of people gathered.

The two friends parted and Lauren began to look for Cathy, Emma, and Katie. The process took longer than she had hoped.

First of all, she had run into her parents. They wanted to know all about the castle, how she was doing, if she made any friends, all that stuff. When she was finally able to leave them, every person around her was saying hello and starting small conversations.

"I love your gown," one girl was saying to Lauren. "I would never be able to afford something that beautiful. But of course, I am poor and you are rich, and the princess deserves the best."

"Well, it was nice talking to you," Lauren said, trying not to sound rude. "I am going to go mingle with all the other people too. You know, got to make room for everyone."

Lauren turned around and began walking away. *Whew!* She thought. *Now, where are those three girls?*

The young princess tried to think and therefore didn't see the young man in front of her.

"Oh! I am so sorry!" Lauren exclaimed, as the boy she had run into wiped off the drink that had been in his glass the moment before.

"It is perfectly all right, Miss," the boy said as he looked up. "Princess Lauren!" He suddenly exclaimed. What a pleasant surprise! I wasn't expecting the young lady herself!"

Lauren smiled. All of a sudden she didn't feel like searching for her friends anymore. Something about this young man absorbed her.

"Where are my manners!?" The boy continued. "My name is Logan. Logan James Ward, and it is a splendid pleasure to meet you, your Highness."

"Please," Lauren said. "Call me Lauren. Just Lauren."

"Of course, Lauren," he said, "with all happiness."

As they looked into each other's eyes, Logan noticed the previous waltz had just finished and an idea popped into his head.

"Lauren, may I have this dance?" He asked.

Lauren blushed, but how could she refuse? "Of course," she said, and curtsied as the next waltz began.

At the edge of the ballroom, their actions did not go unnoticed.

"Darling," Queen Elizabeth said, trying to get the attention of her husband.

"Oh look!" The king said. "There is the royal blacksmith. Doesn't he look nice tonight!"

"Darling!" The queen repeated herself.

"Yes, sweetheart?"

Queen Elizabeth calmed down and pointed to where Logan and Lauren were dancing on the ballroom floor in front of them. "It looks like our new daughter has found a partner."

The king and queen sat quietly on their thrones and watched Logan and Lauren dance the night away.

When the clock struck midnight, it seemed to Lauren that only a few seconds had passed. All the guests began to leave.

"I hate to say this," Logan said, "but I have to go."

Lauren's heart sank. "Will we see each other again?"

"I do not know," Logan replied. "But I promise you, I will come to every party the palace hosts."

"All right then," Lauren said.

She and Logan looked into each other's eyes and hoped with all their hearts that they would see each other again.

———

Dianna yawned. Two weeks had passed since the ball. It all seemed like a dream now.

The two girls dressed and brushed their hair. Then Dianna asked, "Lauren, why don't we go to town today and check out the new beauty shop called Get the Look?"

"Why not?" Lauren replied. "We just have to ask Queen Elizabeth."

They found the queen walking around the throne room.

"Mother," Lauren asked, "May Dianna and I go to town today?"

"Yes, yes, you may," shivered the queen. "It is very cold in here today."

"Would you like some hot tea, your Highness?" Julia asked.

"Yes, thank you, Julia," Queen Elizabeth replied.

Lauren and Dianna gave the queen a look of concern, then smiled at each other and headed out to the courtyard where a stagecoach was waiting for them.

On their way there, Lauren daydreamed about Logan. Would she ever see him again? If so, would it be soon? Lauren hoped with all her heart that the answer to both of those questions was yes.

As she daydreamed, Lauren looked out her window. She noticed that everyone was bowing as the carriage passed. Lauren remembered when she used to bow to the princess. Now she was the princess!

Finally, they arrived. The shop was a place where men and women could get haircuts, shaves, their hair done, nails painted, and enjoy a spa.

As Lauren and Dianna waited in line, she continued to daydream about Logan. While her mind began to float off to another planet, she just happened to begin observing the young man in front of her.

He looked a lot like Logan. He was tall and had coal-black hair.

"Just like Logan's…" she whispered to herself, but then realized she whispered too loud because the young man in front of her turned around.

However, when the young man did turn around, Lauren didn't regret whispering too loud one bit. Why? Because the young man was Logan!

"Lauren!" He exclaimed. "It is nice to see you again. Who is this you have with you?"

"Oh, this is Dianna. She is the queen's niece. Dianna, this is Logan. I met him at the ball."

"Hello," Dianna greeted. As Logan nodded back, Dianna began to understand something special about the two people in front of her.

"Why are you here?" Logan asked Lauren. "Any specific reason?"

"Dianna wanted to check it out," Lauren replied, "and I agreed to come along. Why are you here?"

"Well, it just happens to be that after I was all cleaned up, I was going to stop by the palace and see if you would like to join me for supper tonight."

"Oh," Lauren said, now partly embarrassed.

"If you will excuse me," Dianna said. "I am going to leave you two alone." She then walked over to a shelf of items and pretended to be interested in them.

"Right now," Logan continued, "I'm changing my plans and asking you now. Would you like to join me for supper tonight?"

"I would be honored," Lauren said.

"No," Logan insisted, "*I* would be honored."

———————

A few weeks later, Logan and Lauren were going on a trip with their friends. Cathy, Emma, Katie, the maids Julia and Chrissa, and even some of Logan's friends all gathered at the palace to prepare for their departure. With everything packed and ready to go, the band of them left the next morning.

When they arrived a few hours later at a log cabin, everyone unpacked before spending the rest of the day exploring the area. Logan and Lauren took a walk in the woods and Lauren enjoyed every bit of it. Even the bugs and cold weather didn't bother her much, as long as Logan was there.

The next morning, when Lauren awoke, Logan was nowhere to be found. Emma was in the bathroom, Julia was in the kitchen, Logan's friends were playing cards on the porch, and through the window she could tell Katie had found some chipmunks in the yard. But Lauren didn't see Logan anywhere.

At last, she went to the cabin door, opening it to find Logan just reaching for the doorknob himself.

"Good morning, sweetheart," he said, coming inside. "Did you sleep well?"

"Yes," she replied, closing the door. "Where have you been?"

"This morning when I awoke, seeing that you were still asleep, I went out and did a little Christmas shopping. Because darling, since you most likely forgot, tomorrow is Christmas Eve."

"That time of year already?" Lauren said in shock. "Oh my! It will be my first Christmas as a princess."

"And our first Christmas together," Logan said. "Now," said Logan, setting the two packages he had been holding on the breakfast table. "I want you to open your presents."

"Oh, Logan!" Lauren exclaimed. "You didn't have to get me anything! Besides, I have nothing to give you."

"All I want is your friendship," he said, "now open the gifts."

Lauren obeyed and discovered two new Christmas dresses inside.

"Oh, Logan! They're beautiful!" Lauren exclaimed.

"You're more beautiful," he said. "Try them on."

Lauren giggled, picking up one of the dresses and running to the bathroom.

A little later, as Lauren exhibited the second dress to Logan and the others who glanced up from their preoccupations, they heard dog barks.

Lauren and Logan looked out the cabin window and saw two golden retriever puppies, so they went outside to play with them.

"Lauren," Logan said, as he peeled one of the puppies off of his face, "these dogs look like strays, why don't we bring them home?"

"Yes," Lauren said. "Let us take them home. I'm sure Mother wouldn't mind. I'm going to name this one Coconut."

"Hmm," Logan thought, looking at the other dog. "I'll name this one Honey." And he set the little pup gently onto the snow.

"Come on," Lauren said. "It's chilly out here. Let's go in for some hot cocoa."

"All right," Logan said, noticing the second puppy bounding around the yard. "Come on, Honey," he called, and the golden retriever leapt after him.

Lauren and Logan walked inside, their new royal dogs in pursuit.

Hot cocoa made, Lauren and Logan were sipping away at their drinks when Lauren glanced outside. "Logan, look!" She exclaimed. "It's snowing!"

They and the others gathered around the window excitedly.

"Looks like it's going to be a white Christmas," Logan said, wrapping his arm around Lauren. "Come on, let's go out and enjoy it."

"One moment," Lauren said. "Let me finish my hot cocoa."

"All right," Logan replied. "I'll meet you out there. Come on, Honey!"

Honey bounded after Logan as he ran out the door and the others went back to what they were doing. Lauren began to drink her cocoa faster, burning her tongue many times.

When she finally did finish, Lauren set her cup down and ran for the front door, Coconut at her heels. No sooner had she opened the front door did a snowball come flying at her, striking her right in the face.

"Logan!" Lauren yelled, laughing as she jumped outside and began making her own snowballs.

———————

The next morning, they all packed up and went home.

When they arrived at the castle around noon, everyone was almost done decorating the Christmas tree. After saying goodbye to their friends, Lauren and Logan pitched in too.

There were a lot of decorations, but the tree was soon finished with everyone's help.

Kit, one of the cooks, gave everyone a Christmas cookie and a glass of milk. She didn't forget about the new dogs. Coconut and Honey received some water and dog treats.

After everyone was done with their cookies, the queen walked over to Lauren and Logan and said, "You weren't here when I announced this yesterday, but tomorrow evening I am hosting a Christmas party. If you would like, you can help finish the decorating. Also, those two girls over there, I invited them from a neighboring kingdom. The one with the dark brown hair with red highlights is Rosie, and the one with the long brown hair is Kelly. I advise that you make them feel welcome because they do not know anyone here."

"We will, Mother," Lauren said. "Thank you for informing Logan and me."

"You're welcome, sweetheart," the queen said, walking away to attend to other needs.

"I'm going to say hello to Rosie and Kelly and then I'm going to decorate," Lauren told Logan. "What are you going to do?"

"I have a certain something to attend to out of the palace," Logan said, "but I will be back for supper."

"Oh, what is it?"

"It's a surprise," Logan said. "I promise you'll like it."

"Well then, goodbye," Lauren said.

"Goodbye," Logan answered. "I'll see you tonight."

So everyone in the palace had something to do. The cooks cooked, the maids cleaned, Lauren, Dianna, Rosie, and Kelly decorated, and Logan talked to the king before traveling down to the village to get permission to give Lauren his surprise.

———————

The next evening, the party began.

Lauren was wearing the green dress Logan had given her as an early Christmas present. Logan was very pleased to see her in it.

When all the guests had arrived, everyone was escorted to the dining hall, where the royal Christmas dinner was to be served.

The dinner was like none Lauren had ever seen before. There were all sorts of different types of food, too many for Lauren to even begin listing in her mind, and the table decor reflected so much light that the room seemed to be filled with sunshine.

After supper, all the guests poured into the ballroom to exchange gifts and dance.

"Shall we dance, Logan?" Lauren asked.

"In a minute, dear," he said. "Follow me."

Lauren did, and Logan escorted her to the castle balcony.

They started talking about the party, and Logan told Lauren she had done a wonderful job decorating. Lauren said thank you, they looked into each other's eyes, and that's when Logan said the magic words:

"Lauren, will you marry me?"

Lauren's steady heartbeats became very fast.

Was she dreaming? Did Logan really just ask her to marry him? She couldn't believe what was going on.

"Yes," she stammered, then more sure. "Yes. Yes, of course!"

Logan slid the ring onto Lauren's finger, and Lauren hugged him.

Over the next few moments, they discussed when they would host the wedding. When it was decided, the two parted to entertain the guests.

Lauren stood at the entrance of the ballroom and took a deep breath. Did she really just get engaged? Oh my! She was so excited!

"Lauren!" Dianna exclaimed.

Lauren shook away her daydreams.

"Look who I found!" Dianna said.

"Cathy, Emma, and Katie!" Lauren said. "How did you find them, Dianna? You have never met them before."

"Well," Dianna said. "When you vanished, I began to search for you. As I was walking around, these three came up to me and asked if I had seen you. I replied that I was searching for you and then asked how they knew you. When they explained who they were, I was shocked to discover that these are the three girls you told me about! So we began searching together. That's how I spotted you! By the way, where were you?"

"You are not going to believe this!" Lauren exclaimed. She and her friends huddled closer together.

"What?" Katie asked, getting excited about the way Lauren was blushing and giggling.

"Okay," Lauren said, pulling herself together. "Dianna, do you remember that boy named Logan who we ran into at Get the Look?"

"Yes," Dianna said.

"Well," Lauren continued. "He just proposed to me!"

They all squealed and Queen Elizabeth walked over.

"What is so exciting, girls?" She asked.

"Mother," Lauren said, "I'm engaged!"

"Oh my gracious!" The queen exclaimed. "When did it happen, and to who?"

"To Logan Ward," Lauren said. "He just proposed like two moments ago."

"Oh my!" The queen exclaimed. "This needs to be announced!"

The queen pulled Lauren away from her friends and they fished Logan out of the mob of people. The queen then led them to the throne platform.

She told her husband about the event and was almost through a fit to hear that he already knew. The queen controlled herself, however, and stood calmly on the left side of Lauren while the king stood on Logan's right.

"May I please have everyone's attention!" Boomed the king, and everyone turned to him. "I am proud to announce that this very night, my adopted daughter Lauren Louise Lanford has become engaged to Logan James Ward!"

Everyone applauded and cheered as Logan and Lauren strolled onto the ballroom floor. Lauren floated back to her friends and they arranged that everyone was to come over the next day to discuss the wedding gown.

With that, the guests began to return home.

When everyone had left, Lauren retired to her bedchambers and had Julia bring her a pen and paper. With them, she began to write a letter to her parents.

Dear Father and Mother,

I am excited to say that you are invited to a very special wedding. Mine! You are the first to receive an invitation. The wedding will be held early this spring, and I would be overjoyed if you could stay at the palace until the wedding. I am sure you'll accept.

Your daughter,
-Princess Lauren

The next day the castle was in a bustle.

Everyone was busy doing something. The king and queen were talking about the wedding, Logan and his tailor were planning his outfit, the maids were preparing for all the tasks they were about to receive, and Lauren, Dianna, Chrissa, Cathy, Emma, and Katie were having a little trouble deciding what Lauren's wedding dress was going to look like.

"I think it should be orange," Chrissa said.

"Orange is too vibrant," Dianna said. "I think it should be green."

"Both of those colors are way too 'boy,'" Lauren said. "I know that it should be pink."

"I'm going with Lauren," Katie said. "Pink is my favorite color."

"Thank you," Lauren said.

"Well," Emma said, "you can put 'boy' and 'girl' into the dress with purple."

"No way," Cathy said. "None of those colors will do. Gold is so the answer, it will rock your wedding."

They kept discussing, none aware that the whole time, on the other side of the door, Rosie and Kelly had been listening to the whole conversation.

The two girls talked over the problem, and when they had a solution, Rosie opened the door.

"Lauren," Rosie said.

"Yes!" Lauren said, a little worked up.

"I don't think you know this," Rosie continued, "But Kelly and I are the best dress designers in our kingdom."

"So can you help us?" Chrissa asked.

"Well," Kelly said, "Rosie and I were thinking that you could have dark pink cloth on the bottom half of the dress and light pink on the top half."

"To spice it up," Rosie added, "you could have light green, dark pink, and gold ribbon sewn around the waist, along with some light pink and purple flowers sewn onto the side of it."

"To spice it up even more," Kelly continued, "you could wear gold and purple jewelry, white shoes, and a light pink veil with small dark pink, orange, and purple gems sewn on."

"Just perfect!" Lauren exclaimed.

"It has all of our ideas!" Chrissa said.

"You girls *are* the best dressmakers!" Cathy said.

"We're not only the best dressmakers," Rosie said, giving Kelly a hug. "We are best friends!"

The group of girls began measuring Lauren, figuring out how much cloth they would need to purchase, where they would get it, how many fake flowers would have to be made, and how many small gems of each of the picked colors would have to be bought.

During this process, Julia walked in. "Princess Lauren," she said, "your parents are here."

"Thank you," Lauren said. "Will you tell Logan to meet them at the door?"

"Yes, Lauren," Julia answered, as she made her way out the door. "I will."

Lauren turned back to her friends and said, "This is all we'll do today girls. Let's meet here again tomorrow. Right now I have to go greet my parents."

They exchanged farewells and Lauren skipped merrily down the central staircase.

When she reached the courtyard, she found Logan and her parents talking.

When her mother saw her, she walked over and hugged her. "He is wonderful!" She said.

Lauren and Logan showed her parents to their room and then retired to the gardens to take an evening stroll.

Logan and Lauren were very happy.

About three months later, the day before the wedding had arrived. At last.

Rosie and Kelly had finished Lauren's dress, and it looked lovely. The gown looked even better when it was on the bride herself. Of course, Lauren looked beautiful in the dress.

Since Cathy, Emma, and Katie couldn't all be one bridesmaid, Lauren chose Dianna to be her bridesmaid. Since all of her friends were too old to be cute little flower girls, Lauren picked the king's four-year-old twin granddaughters to do the job.

Lauren had wanted to have the wedding in the garden, but it was still cold and the flowers had not yet bloomed, so the princess had sadly planned to wed in the royal chapel. This made the king and queen very happy because they didn't want the wedding to be held in the garden.

When the fairies heard about Lauren's dismay, they built a glass dome over the garden and woke up all of the flowers. Then they enchanted the king and queen to agree with Lauren.

Everything was wonderful.

The next day, all the guests began to arrive. There were more people coming to the wedding than anyone had ever seen before.

Lauren and Logans' parents were coming. The king's first daughter, her husband, and their twin girls were coming. All the king and queen's relatives were coming, which included Dianna's family. Rosie and Kelly invited their families. All of the palace maids and fairies were going to attend. On top of that, everyone in the kingdom was invited, which included Cathy, Emma, and Katie. So as you can see, there were a lot of guests.

Lauren stood outside the dome and watched her cousins stroll down the aisle, tossing rose petals into the air as they went. What everyone didn't know was that the rose petals were magic petals, created by the fairies. Though everyone realized that when the petals hit the dirt path because they hooked together to form a cohesive red carpet.

When the twins reached the end of the aisle, Lauren took a deep breath and began to walk down herself. Before she knew it, the priest was announcing them married.

For the rest of the day, and deep into the night, everyone celebrated.

When the party ended, all the guests departed, and Logan and Lauren strolled happily up to their room. The next day they would travel to their honeymoon destination. It happened to be the kingdom Rosie and Kelly came from.

———————

The next day, Lauren and Logan rode in the stagecoach from their kingdom to the sea. There they would board a ship that would take them to the neighboring kingdom.

Lauren looked out the window at all the people lining their route to the docks and sighed. "Sometimes I wish I could be an ordinary girl again," she said. "Always being the center of attention can get a little tiring."

"Don't stress yourself, Darling," Logan said. "People won't know who you are in the neighboring kingdom. You can relax."

"You're right," Lauren answered.

When they arrived at the inn they were going to stay at, they strolled inside to register.

"This is a beautiful inn," Lauren told the man at the desk.

"Thank you, Madame," he replied.

"We would like to rent your wedding suite please," Logan said.

The man wrote it down in his book as Logan set some money on the counter. "What names shall I put it under?" He asked.

"Mr. and Mrs. Ward," Logan answered, grinning at Lauren.

The man handed them a key and said, "Room 113. Take the stairs there, and when you reach the cafe upstairs, turn right. At the end of that hallway, turn right again. Your room is at the end of the hall on the right."

They said thank you and then headed upstairs.

The luggage they had brought was already there.

"Why don't you freshen up?" Logan said to his lovely bride. "Then we can change for supper and find out where the food is around here."

"I'm up for that," Lauren said, and she began to freshen herself up.

A little later, the couple set out to find food and discovered that meals in their inn were served in the cafe. After a hearty serving of spaghetti and breadsticks, Logan and Lauren turned in for the night.

The next afternoon, the young couple began their tour of the kingdom. At a bulletin board covered in posters for all kinds of events, Logan discovered an ice-skating musical was being held that evening.

"Why don't we attend it, Lauren?" He asked.

"Attend what, Darling?" She replied.

"The skating show tonight," he said, pointing to the poster.

"It sounds like fun," she said. "Why not? I don't believe that I've ever been to one of those."

That evening, Logan and Lauren could have been found watching hundreds of elegant ice skaters. They watched them spin, flip, and dance across the ice.

"My!" Lauren exclaimed in a whisper to Logan. "Aren't they talented?"

"Yes, they are," Logan replied. "You were right. This is a lot of fun."

A few days later, the young couple returned home. Once settled in, the king and queen wanted to know if Lauren was going to move to another castle like their first daughter did.

"I will remain in this palace," Lauren answered, "and our children will be the heirs of your throne."

Her adoptive parents were very pleased to hear this.

Lauren and Logan had a very happy marriage and were soon the parents of two girls, Faith and Hope, born about a year apart from each other.

"They're beautiful," Lauren whispered as she and Logan gazed down at the two girls asleep in their cradle.

"One day they will do *exactly* what we did," Logan said. "They'll grow up, they'll fall in love, and they will get married."

Lauren smiled, it was true. Their baby girls would be grown up one day. She decided right then and there that she would treasure every moment to come.

Nature Royalty

Once upon a time, there lived a king and his lovely queen. They were the rulers of all of nature. High King Buffalo ruled over all of the animals while his wife, High Queen Strawberry, looked after all of the plants. Together the couple made sure the seasons came and left on time.

The King and Queen had always wanted a child. One fall morning, the royal family was blessed with a baby girl. They named her Princess Eversun and, as years passed, she grew up to be a tall and fair young lady.

When Princess Eversun came of age, the king and queen recognized that their daughter had grown in quality and character, so they made her queen of the land. In the beginning, High King Buffalo and High Queen Strawberry assisted their daughter's rule over all of nature, but soon they passed the full responsibility on to her.

The new queen had lots to do. First of all, she had to look after the plants and animals, then she had to make sure the seasons came and went at the correct times. She also had to make sure nothing odd happened, like waves so big they surpassed the shore. That may not seem like a lot, but it is a handful for one queen to do. The most obvious answer was to find a husband to be her partner, but Queen Eversun was not interested in marriage.

One day the young queen noticed that orphan girls were visiting the palace and an idea came to her: she could adopt four daughters to look after each season for her. Of course! It was an excellent plan. Right away the queen set out to determine soon-to-be princesses.

In due time, Queen Eversun had adopted four daughters: Forget-Me-Not, the princess of spring, Rose, the princess of summer, Daisy, the princess of fall, and Blue Bell, the princess of winter.

Queen Eversun saw that her newly adopted daughters were young and not capable of protecting themselves, so she went in search of suitable guardians who could protect her daughters from any danger.

Soon the young queen had the guardians she needed. First of all, there was Guardian Rex for Princess Forget-Me-Not and then Guardian Rhino for Princess Rose. Guardian Panda was the guardian of Princess Daisy and Guardian Cheetah was the guardian of Princess Blue Bell.

There was one guardian in training and that was Guardian Panda's younger brother. His name was Panther.

As for Queen Eversun, she could take care of herself but decided to also appoint her own guardian. She chose Guardian Wolf, guardian of the mighty Queen Eversun.

The new guardians had lots to learn, like some self-control because it was getting on the princesses' nerves, like how they just strolled into the ladies' quarters and touched whatever they pleased.

That needs to be worked on, thought Queen Eversun, so she decided to start a little school. She would be the teacher and make sure her students learned everything they needed to know about being a royal guardian or princess. High King Buffalo and High Queen Strawberry were in support of this idea and helped bear some of the kingdom's responsibilities so she could attend to her pupils.

But where was she to start? From tea party etiquette to ballroom dancing and fencing to the best armor-cleaning practices, there was so much to teach. And that was just the beginning. Each princess also needed to learn how to take care of the plants. Finally, the young queen decided to start with how to address a queen.

First, she explained the process to her four daughters and then had them take turns leaving the room so they could practice an initial address.

Princess Forget-Me-Not went first. She walked outside the queen's room and closed the door. Inside, three knocks could be heard.

"Who is it?" Queen Eversun asked.

"Forget-Me-Not," came an answer.

"Princess Forget-Me-Not," the queen corrected.

"Oops!" Forget-Me-Not said and tried again. "Princess Forget-Me-Not."

"Come in," the queen said, setting her paintbrush down on a tray connected to her easel with vines.

Princess Forget-Me-Not opened the door, stepped inside, forgot to close the door, and walked over to her mother. Curtsying, she said, "My queen."

Queen Eversun smiled and said, "Speak."

"I don't know what to say," she answered.

"That's fine," her mother replied. "Daisy, you're next."

Princess Daisy went outside and repeated the process her sister had just completed. She also forgot to say "princess" but remembered to close the door.

"Speak," the queen said as Princess Daisy rose from her curtsey.

Daisy began to laugh and said, "Blah, blah, blah. Blah, blah. Blah, blah."

She sat down on her mother's bed and Blue Bell slid off, landing safely on the floor. The little princess went outside her mother's door and began the same process her sisters had.

When her mother told her to speak, she clasped her hands together, brought them up to her face, and said in the sweetest voice, "Mother, someone broke into the jewelry room."

Everyone burst out in laughter and Queen Eversun picked the young princess up and swirled her around saying, "Oh, Blue Bell! You're so charming!"

The schooling was obviously over and they went out for a walk. Here, the guardians joined them and Queen Eversun taught everyone the correct walking formation.

"I am standing here," the queen said, "and my daughters are to line up—in birth order—behind my left arm. The guardians are to stand beside their princess so they form a line behind my right arm."

The guardians and princesses did as instructed.

There, that wasn't too hard, the young queen thought. "If I am to stop," she continued, "the princesses are to fan out in birth order on my left side and their guardians are to mirror them on my right side."

Again they obeyed and easily understood how the process was to work. The queen was very pleased.

After their walk, it was decided that it had been a healthy day. Lots taught, lots learned. However, there was much more Queen Eversun needed to teach her young daughters.

She sighed and watched the dismissed children play around the yard. She would be able to teach them and they would grow up into beautiful young ladies ruling over the seasons as princesses should.

Adah

The sky was cloudless, allowing the sun to beat mercilessly on the children of Judea. Behind them, their homes lay in ruins and fires burned everywhere. Around them, Babylonian guards circled little groups of family and friends, huddled together crying.

One by one the Jewish captives were roughly examined. Any wounded or weak captives were eliminated, an awful sight that made every step the guards took send a shiver up Adah's body.

"It will be all right," Zachariah said, wrapping an arm around his wife's shoulder. "God is with us."

Adah tried to smile, then wrapped her arm around their daughter.

Adah looked around. It was almost unbearable to watch her friends and neighbors get beaten, children ripped from their parents, and husbands peeled from their wives. Tears began to flow as Adah recalled her own parents and siblings being killed shortly before her family was forced out of the city. God had spared their lives, but now they were captives.

"Bring them to me!" Ordered a Chaldean.

Adah jumped. He was looking right at her. Before she could begin to panic, a guard grabbed her arm while another gripped Zachariah and simultaneously forced them toward the Chaldean.

The Chaldean motioned for Zachariah to be removed and the second guard thrust him away from Adah.

"No!" Adah screamed, reaching for him.

The first guard rushed forward and grabbed her outstretched arm before shoving her aside and standing between her and Zachariah.

Tears streamed from Adah's eyes and she wrapped her arms around her daughter.

Stepping closer, the Chaldean grabbed Adah's face and stared coldly into her eyes. After quickly examining her, he tore Adah's arms off her daughter and looked the child over.

"They are in perfect shape," the Chaldean said. "Lucky for them," he grumbled, walking away as the guard shoved Zachariah back to his family.

Adah grabbed his hand and interlaced her fingers with his as the guard thrust their little family toward the other

captives. Then the guards began to shove them all
onward— to Babylon.

Adah approached the large, liquid-filled vessel and was
immediately captured by the sight of her reflection within.
From getting ready that morning, she had a conceptual idea
of what she must look like, but the holistic picture staring
back now took her by surprise.

Her hair had been curled, the sides pinned back, and a gold
headband placed on top. Black eyeliner made small
rectangles that protruded from her eyes. She was wearing a
purple tunic and coordinating sash. Her sandals were
covered in metal pieces that had been sewn into a
geometric pattern.

There was almost nothing to recognize of the scared, young
mother who had been removed from her homeland three
years prior. She had been given a new name, ate a daily
portion of the king's food, and could now speak the
language of the Chaldeans. Her education was complete
and today she was beginning her role as a wine bearer.

Adah broke the surface of the wine and filled her jar.

She did not know where her husband had been taken but
looked for him daily among the bustling halls of the palace.
Even now, as she dashed amongst the swarms of other
servants preparing for another of the king's feasts, she
hoped to catch sight of him.

She was rounding a corner when she thought she recognized Zachariah's silhouette. Another wave of disappointment began to set in as she recognized yet another mistake, but all such thoughts were jolted from her mind as she bumped into someone coming the opposite way.

Securing her jar from spilling any of its contents, she looked up to recognize Ashpenaz, the king's chief eunuch, and immediately fell into a stance of reference. "Most solemn of apologies," she said in Aramaic. "Please forgive my carelessness."

"Nothing to forgive, Anatu," he said, using her new name as he returned her to an upright position. "There is always so much going on in these halls during feast time. Maybe I should appeal to the king about expanding the kitchens to match the size of his parties."

Adah forced a small laugh and they continued on their ways.

Ashpenaz was the one the king had charged to select Israeli youths of good appearance and sound minds to serve in the king's court. Adah's daughter had been among them. Adah occasionally saw her at the meals she served, but their contact was limited to the distant meeting of their eyes and encouraging smiles. Adah prayed for her daily.

That was about all she could do. The ultimate goal of the Babylonians' transformation was to abolish their religion and all others like it. Adah and her fellow captives could worship their God in private as long as they accepted the Babylonian gods in public.

This was perhaps the loneliest thing of all.

There was no one with whom Adah could have reciprocal encouragement. Zachariah was so good at lifting her spirits and keeping her mind focused on what really mattered, but now Adah found herself having to stand such ground alone.

Where were the judges of old? Where were the prophets sent by God? Why were there no leaders to stand up against the contrary beliefs they were bowing down to?

———————

Whether Ashpenaz put through a request about expanding the kitchens or not, Adah did not know. Regardless, construction did begin, but not in the palace. Across the way, in the plain of Dura, a statue of the king was built. It was bigger than anything Adah had ever seen before and impossible to miss with how its gold, silver, and bronze plates caught the sunlight. She didn't understand how one could possess so much wealth that sums of it could be molded together for public display.

Shortly after the statue was dedicated to the king, Adah again found the halls crowded with people, but this time they weren't hurriedly moving about. Everyone was creating a semi-circle around one point on the wall, craning to see what others blocked from view and whispering amongst themselves. Adah caught sight of the object in question, an official notice, but also found herself too far away to make out what it said.

"What is it?" She asked a cluster of servants in front of her.

"A decree," one replied. "It says, when we hear music, we are to fall down and worship the statue of the king. Anyone who doesn't will be thrown into a fiery furnace."

"Oh," Adah said. "Thank you," and she continued on her way, a confusing tangle of emotions twisting about in her stomach.

She grieved the lack of acknowledgment for the one true God and was struck with guilt of how less and less of her was proclaiming His presence as Babylonian customs took over her existence. She shouldn't bow down. She wouldn't. But she had to. Love for her daughter and husband swelled within her and the hope that they would one day be reunited proclaimed that she must stay alive. So, wherever the music found her, Adah bowed down.

At first, she left a small puddle of tears where her forehead had been pressed to the earth, but then she began to leave a piece of herself behind as well.

Who was to say that the faith of her ancestors was more than just a collection of stories? What made the God of Moses any more real than the gods of Babylonians? On and on the questions taunted until Adah felt like a shell of another person carrying out strange customs in a foreign country.

Adah again found herself alone in the wine cellar. Her jar was in hand, but she only stared into the wine-filled vat.

She had gone through that day's call to worship without thought, just the motions. She was numb to everything else. She didn't even look up when someone came barreling down the hall outside, working everyone up into hoops and hollers of joy. Maybe they were getting a kitchen expansion after all.

Suddenly the causing force burst in. "Adah!" A male voice exclaimed.

"It's Anatu," she replied, still not looking up.

"Adah!" The voice called again, its source suddenly right beside her, removing her jar from her hands so she'd look up at—

"Zachariah?" Adah hardly whispered. She didn't know what to think, she hardly believed what she was seeing. It couldn't be. Was it really him?

"Yes!" Her husband replied. "It's really me, and I've come to tell you that salvation has come! The king found out that three of our own have been refusing to bow down to his statue, so they were thrown into the fiery furnace, but not a hair burned! God Himself met them in the fire! He delivered them from the flames, and the king saw it! He completely reversed his decree, proclaiming that there is no other God like our God and that anyone who says anything against Him will be destroyed. Adah, my love, all has been set right!"

Adah just stared at him, trying to wrap her mind around it all. "Really?" She asked.

"Yes!" Zachariah exclaimed. "I was there! I saw it all myself and ran to find you as soon as the king issued his decree. Rightful worship has been restored!"

Adah spit up a laugh. Her God, her husband, her people, all being set right. It was too much joy to bear and she began to cry.

Zachariah pulled her into his arms and held her close. "Come," he said, kissing her head. "Let's go find our daughter. Today is indeed a happy day!"

The Mysterious Figure

Co-Authored by Abigayle Moran

Who am I? My name is Elizabeth Claire Wright, but my friends call me Claire. I am the super forgetful, terribly clumsy, overthinking ninth-grader who— Never mind, let's just get to the story.

I took the money, stuffed the ham and cheese— This is not it, let me go back a few pages. Ah! Here it is. I noticed a dark-clothed figure— Where is the beginning? Let me turn back a few more pages. This has to be it.

As I rushed to my home one late August day, I knew I had forgotten something. I had left my physical science homework at home! (This is definitely it.)

It was only my second week in high school and I had already become known for my forgetfulness. "But today," I had told myself. "I will not forget anything."

I knew it was wishful thinking. I always forget something. One of these days I'm going to end up leaving my book bag at home.

I realized my mistake partway through lunch. Since I live right down the street, I got permission from the lunch supervisor to run home.

I am a pretty fast runner, thanks to my long legs. If you didn't know me well, you would think I'm a marathoner. I can run up to four miles before I get tired. Of course, I have had a lot of practice. I just recently became able to beat my younger brothers in a race. This thought caused me to pick up my speed a bit, and then I ran into someone.

"Hey, what are you running for, Rapid?" It was my dad, out on his usual afternoon walk. I love the little nicknames he gives me. Like Browny, because my eyes are brown, or Rosy because my cheeks are rosy red. It helps me not worry about how I look.

"Hi, Dad!" I greeted as he pulled me into a hug. He smelled like coffee.

He and Mom work at a coffee shop, so he's there a lot. He works more hours than Mom so she can be home more often. What he doesn't know is that Mom would rather work there than at home.

"I left my homework at home, again," I explained, releasing my hug.

"Oh, all right," he said, chuckling. "Better hurry along now, don't want to be late."

As I ran into the neighborhood, I turned left and passed our neighbor's house. We didn't really get to know them until the man passed away. Since then, we often visit his widow. She loves children. I think it's partly because her two sons are grown and have moved out.

I have nine younger siblings, all of which are a year apart. Our four-bedroom house landed three kids per room: JJ (John Jr.), Heidi, and me; James, Lily, and Jack; then Jo (Jolene), Josh, and Jacob. Laura Lou, the baby of the family, sleeps in our parents' room. Laura Lou, oh how she tries to help. Yes, she's cute and all, but sometimes she just gets in the way.

I ran up the front porch steps and through the front door. Mom was seated at the island in the kitchen eating lunch. Startled, she looked up. Seeing it was me, she asked, "Forget your homework again, Claire?"

"Yep!" I said, running up to my room and snatching the papers that lay abandoned on my desk.

As I returned downstairs, I found Mom had left the island to close the door I had carelessly left open. I love my mom. She's always there for me whenever I'm stressed or troubled. It's as if she's saying, "You're doing great."

"Sorry!" I called as I dashed out the half-closed door, startling Mom again.

She recovered quickly and stepped onto the front porch, smiling. "See you later, Sweetie!" She called and then watched me until I had rounded the corner and was out of sight.

When I reached the four-way stop, the light was red, so I bent down to tie my shoe. Knowing how clumsy I am, I would trip and fall if I were to keep running with a dangling shoelace.

When I stood back up, I noticed a mysterious figure walking down the sidewalk across the street. He, or she, was wearing a black hoodie and sunglasses.

I gazed at the figure, wondering who he or she was. Then the signal change reminded me I was running late, so I jumped up and ran across the street.

When I finally reached my locker, the fourth-period bell rang. The halls quickly cleared as I piled what I needed into my arms. Upon closing my locker (a bit louder than I intended), I raced through the halls, imagining my best friend Kristina nervous that I wouldn't make it due to an accident that would terrify first responders.

I raced into my Physical Science classroom and plopped into my seat next to Kristina. She, as usual, was as calm as can be (so much for my overactive imagination).

My classmates, busy scribbling down the few lines of notes our teacher had already begun writing out for us to copy, were already used to me dashing in like this, so only a few glanced up. Most didn't bother.

Mr. Hardyman wasn't so forgiving. "Elizabeth," I heard my teacher call.

I looked up at him. He is not one of my favorite teachers. In fact, I hardly tolerate him enough to stand his class, which is not very much. It is because of him that Physical Science is my least favorite class. He is very strict and seems to enjoy putting students down to make himself look better.

"Would you care to hand in yesterday's homework?" He asked. "The homework your classmates have already supplied for me."

One of the meaner kids snickered. "Most of them," he said, motioning with his pencil to a rather pale kid—Collin, I think his name is—who had apparently received quite the deduction for arriving in class without his homework.

A few people chuckled.

"Silence!" Mr. Hardyman bellowed and everyone in the room became still, though some had to clasp their hands over their mouths. Mr. Hardyman turned back to me. "Well, would you like to give me your homework?" He asked. "Or have you forgotten it…again?" He clearly expected me to be ashamed or embarrassed for the homework he was sure I had forgotten.

I smiled sweetly and handed him the stack of paper I had set on my desk. I thought I saw some surprise in his expression, but he seemed to have moved on to a suddenly needed plan B.

Mr. Hardyman took the stack, smiling wickedly at me, and then began to flip through the papers. His expression grew more unpleasant with each page. After scanning the last, he looked back up at me, not pleased.

He moved back to his desk and opened his attendance book. "Elizabeth Wright," He said, picking up a pen and writing something in the book. "Late to class. That gives you yet another tardy mark. Any more from you, young lady, and you will receive an after-school detention."

"I'm glad that's over," I said as Kristina and I walked out from another day of school and into the heat of the outside.

Kristina began to say something in reply but, to me, her voice quickly faded away as I noticed the dark-clothed stranger from earlier.

He (I'm positive it's a he) was walking along the sidewalk across the street from the parking lot where he turned into the neighborhood there. I watched him go.

"Claire?" Kristina's voice suddenly came back to me. "Claire!"

I snapped out of my daze. "Oh, sorry. What?"

"Your mom's here," she told me.

"Oh, okay," I said, suddenly seeing our van in the car line in front of me. "See you later!" I called and scrambled in the open side door where my siblings were impatiently waiting.

By the time we were home, the after-school daze had come over me. I was the last one out of the van and took my time to grab a snack and head up to my room.

My siblings were the complete opposite. They dashed upstairs for a few moments of playtime before Mom would inevitably remind them of a chore they needed to do.

Upon entering my room, I dropped my backpack in a chair and collapsed onto my bed. I lay there for a few moments and then reached under my pillow and pulled out my Bible. I keep it there to help me remember to read it, but I always forget anyway. I opened it to the center and tried to focus on the words, but my mind kept drifting to the stranger.

Finally, I gave up and set the holy book on my nightstand. Questions began popping into my head: *Who is this guy? A stalker? What is he like? Does he plan to hurt me? Will he continue to follow me? What if he's my secret admirer?* This thought amused me. To think that someone would secretly be head over heels in love with the likes of me…

It seemed like only a few minutes when JJ, James, Jack, Joshua, and Jacob came in to tickle me awake (it's the morning routine). Apparently I had fallen asleep and slept through the entire night.

After a few groans of, "I'm up, I'm up," they left to go wake up the other girls.

Blurry-eyed, I looked around my room. Then it occurred to me, *I didn't do my homework! What am I going to do? I always forget something! I always have and I always will. This isn't gonna —*

"We're going to Grandma's!" Little Jacob exclaimed.

It was Saturday. I didn't have any homework. I completely forgot.

Tummy rumbling, I ran downstairs and put together some breakfast. I was getting ready to take a bite when something caught my eye through the front window.

I jumped out of my seat. There was the stranger! He was jogging by. *Must be on a morning run,* I thought as I dashed outside, but he had already passed.

"Claire?" Mom called. "What are you doing?"

"Uh," I thought fast. The dog, yes. "Checking on Oscar," I replied. "I think I forgot to feed him yesterday."

"I took care of it," she said. "But, sweetie, Oscar's pen is in the backyard."

"Yeah... But, you know, I just woke up and had a mini heart attack so I, uh, wasn't thinking very clearly." I nervously laughed and quickly made my way back inside, ignoring the worried expression on Mom's face.

The drive to our grandparents' house was pretty dull. Lily, Jack, and Jo were trying to play a three-way battle of "rock, paper, scissors." Laura Lou and Jacob were trying to copy whatever move Jo was making. Meanwhile, Heidi and Josh were having a conversation about sports cars. As for James and JJ— well, they were playing on their tablets. So, as usual, that left me alone.

When we finally arrived at my grandparents' house, I gave them a hug before the "grown-ups" slipped into conversation and I fell back to pondering the stranger.

He's starting to creep me out, I thought.

As of yesterday morning, I had never seen him before and now he was everywhere. What could this mean? Would I ever know? What if the stranger was trying to find my identity? What if—

"There he is!" I shouted, pointing to a dark-clothed figure walking down the street, then realized, upon second glance, it was just a neighbor taking an afternoon stroll.

My family stared at me as if I was crazy. Am I crazy? Yes, but not this crazy.

"Who wants some freshly baked pie?" My grandmother asked.

At the very word "pie," everyone got up and ran toward the kitchen. Grandma asked me to help her serve.

———————

Because of my not-so-little outburst over the stranger, Mom thought I was sick, so she took me to the medical center after church the next day. Of course, the doctor found nothing wrong with me, but my overprotective mother kept thinking of things for him to look into, so we were there until late afternoon.

When we walked out of the lobby into the depressing rainy day, we were unsuccessful at trying to dodge the precipitation on the way to our car. We would have taken the van, but Dad used it to take the others out to lunch.

"Are you hungry?" Mom asked, 10 minutes later, as she opened our front door.

I trudged inside. "No. I think I'll go take a nap," I said, sighing as I began to climb the spiral staircase that led upstairs.

It is not like me to decide to take a nap instead of eating lunch, but I was tired because I stayed up late last night thinking about the mysterious figure. I knew I should have gone to sleep, but I couldn't help myself. I wandered into my room and, upon collapsing onto my bed, fell asleep.

I awoke to smacking lips. It was Jo finishing off her leftovers. We are not allowed to have food upstairs, but I was too tired to lecture her.

"Jack says you got issues," she stated after swallowing a mouthful of french fries.

"I don't have issues," I mumbled, sitting up.

"Then why did mom take you to the doctor?"

"Because of my little outburst yesterday."

"What's an outburst?" Jo asked.

"An outburst is a sudden release of strong emotion," I stated, quite pleased that I actually remembered the definition.

"What were you emotional about?" She asked in her I'm-smarter-than-you voice.

"Well," I started, "Friday I saw this guy dressed in dark clothing and then yesterday morning he was jogging by the house. I was thinking about him at Grandpa and Grandma's when I thought I saw him walking down the street. Turns out it was just some random dude. I guess mom thought I was crazy, so she took me to see a doctor. Do you think I'm crazy?"

Jo shrugged her shoulders. "If crazy means you forget stuff all the time, see weird guys everywhere, and have outbursts— yes."

I was rather offended by her answer and was therefore glad mom called her to help James empty the dishwasher. Jo obeyed, though she left the room muttering something about it not being her turn.

When she was gone, I sighed and fell back onto my bed, accidentally banging my head against my headboard. "Ow!" I exclaimed, rubbing my skull. Why can't I get it through my head that life is not like the movies? I slowly placed myself in a comfortable position and fell asleep wondering who the stranger could be.

———————

Beep! Beep! Beep! Was the first sound I heard Monday morning.

I quickly stuffed my things into my backpack and began to do my make-up. That is one of the few things I can do well. Whenever my friends come over they usually ask me to do theirs. They say I'm really good, which I guess I am, but when I grow up I want to do something with animals, not cosmetology.

Applying some chapstick, I had a feeling that I had forgotten something…again.

"Claire!" Mom called up the stairs. "We're leaving!"

"Coming!" I yelled, as I stuffed the tube of chapstick into my pocket and slung the backpack over my shoulder.

I rushed down the stairs and was halfway through the kitchen when, from the corner of my eye, I caught sight of my lunchbox. I had forgotten to pack my lunch.

As I began digging through the fridge for the ham and cheese, Mom came out of Dad's office, the car keys jingling in her hand. "What are you doing, Claire?" She asked as she grabbed her purse off of the island. "We have to go."

"I forgot to pack my lunch," I said, bringing the ham and cheese over to the counter.

"You don't have time to pack a lunch, unless you plan to run to school," she teased as she dug through her purse. She pulled out a five-dollar bill. "Here. You can buy lunch at school today. Now come on, we're already running late."

I took the money, stuffed the ham and cheese back into the fridge, and followed her into the garage where I squeezed into the van with my siblings.

"Guess what we have to do for English?" I told Kristina, as we stuffed our books into our lockers.

"Something you're about to complain to me about?" She teased, grabbing her lunch bag and closing her locker door.

"We have to write a super essay so 'super,'" I said, making air quotes, "that the outline is two pages long," I whined, closing my locker with more force than I meant to use so it shut with a loud *BANG!*

I cringed and tried to avoid the fact that everyone in the hall was now staring at me as Kristina and I made our way to the cafeteria.

"I thought you liked writing," Kristina reminded me. She was always looking for the bright side in dull situations.

"I do," I agreed. "It's just that English is SO tedious."

"One day you will be a famous author and we'll be eating lunch in some fancy restaurant as you tell me how happy you are that you took English and 'suffered' through whatever it is you're calling tedious."

I smiled. "You're probably right," I said as we entered the cafeteria. "You go to our table," I told Kristina. "My mom said I can buy lunch today."

"Let me guess," she said in a teasing tone again, "you forgot to pack yours."

"I wonder how you guessed that?" I laughed as I made my way to the lunch bar.

I got in line behind a boy I hadn't seen before, and yet, something about him reminded me of the stranger. This, of course, sent thoughts flying through my head again.

I slid a tray off the big stack that sat on the counter and placed it on the rack. "Who is the mysterious figure?" I whispered to myself.

"What?" Asked the new boy, turning to me. He was skinny, had brown hair, and was a bit taller than me.

I blushed. "Nothing."

"No, really, what?" He insisted.

Surprised, I looked into his eyes. They were sepia brown and gave a glint of humor now. Despite the situation, I found myself noticing how they seemed to twinkle.

I don't know what it was—maybe the fact that he seemed to actually care about what I had to say, or the way I suddenly felt comfortable around him (when with other boys I am a nervous wreck)—but something about him caused me to share about the stranger.

He grinned throughout my short story as we each grabbed our lunch and then paid for it at the register. "Anyway, I can't get this creepy whoever-he-is off my mind and my family thinks I'm going crazy."

It was then that he began to laugh.

"What?" I asked, startled by the sudden change of mood.

"I just so happen to be the 'mysterious figure,'" he laughed.

"What!?"

He smiled and then explained that he had just moved here. After settling in, he was bored and so decided to dress up in a creepy way and walk around. He was on a jog when I saw him Saturday, as I suspected. "I'm sorry if I creeped you out," he said.

"No, no, that's fine," I said, suddenly feeling rather clear-headed. "I'm Claire, by the way."

"Nick," he replied.

It was then that I glanced at Kristina, who was watching Nick and me from our table, and I realized that lunch must be half over and I hadn't even begun my meal. "I have to go," I told my new friend. "See you around?"

"Yeah," he replied. "See you around." Then he joined a table full of boys while I reunited with Kristina.

"Claire has a crush!" She sang quietly in my ear as I sat down next to her.

"I do not!" I said, feeling my cheeks turning red. I glanced over at Nick. "We're just new…acquaintances."

Little did I know, that meeting in the cafeteria on a usual
Monday afternoon was the beginning of the best thing that
has ever happened to Elizabeth Claire Wright.

The Kidnapped Princess

Tara was a detective. She helped many different kinds of people with their mysteries. Most of the time she was at the police station helping the policemen solve their crimes. But other times, she was helping neighbors and friends find a missing cat or other belongings.

While Tara was solving mysteries, she was attracting young men like a magnet. Tara constantly had these men coming to her house to ask if she would like to go on a date. But Tara never found any of them interesting and turned their offers down.

With all the attention, Tara's routine was to clean her house often. Saturday was her "clean the house" day.

One Saturday morning, Tara woke up and started cleaning as usual. Little did she know, that was the day the biggest and most interesting mystery of her life would begin.

Tara was sweeping around her bed when she noticed a floorboard that had popped out. She tried to push it down, but it would not go down.

There must be something under this board that is holding it up, she thought.

Tara pulled the board up and put a book under the board to hold it. Then she got her torch (flashlight) and looked under the plank. Tara was right, underneath the plank was an old wooden box.

Tara pulled the box out and then opened it. Inside there were two old and wrinkled papers. She examined them. One paper was an old map of the Persian Empire. The other paper had the words: *Princess Tara of Persia.*

Tara stared at the paper. *How in the world – ?* She thought. *Could I have the same name as this princess who lived long ago?*

She put the papers back in the box, the plank back on the floor, and got up and walked to the library.

When Tara got to the library, she found a book called *The Dynasty of Persia.* Tara looked through the contents until she found what she was looking for. Tara turned to the chapter called, "Princess Tara of Persia." This is what she read:

Princess Tara was kidnapped one night from the Persian palace located next to the black sea. No one knows who kidnapped her because no one at the palace realized she was gone until the next morning. Tara was about 15 years old.

But historians do know that while in captivity, she married and gave birth to a son. They know this because the son, Prince Alek, was returned to the palace one night when he was five years old. The palace maid found him sleeping in Princess Tara's bed. Since he was so young, he did not know that his parents were captives, who captured them, or where they were. The only thing he did know was that his mother's name was Tara and his father's name was also Alek.

Tara stopped reading and turned her attention to the map. It showed the Red Sea and the Black Sea. Then a sudden thought struck Tara's mind: *Maybe Princess Tara was kidnapped by pirates.*

Tara thought that it made sense. Her palace was next to the sea which would make it very easy for pirates to sneak into the palace and leave before anyone noticed.

I don't know why the seas would make me think that… Tara mused. Oh, wait! Maybe the pirates later conquered the Persian Empire and threatened everyone so no one was able to pass down the story. And then Tara's son left a clue by naming the seas pirate colors. That way the pirates would never find out that he left a passage of hope for the mystery to be solved! And then later he must have escaped to another country — but the book said he didn't know. Maybe he didn't tell. Maybe he just kept it a secret because, if he could remember his parents' names, I'm sure he could remember something else. Tara was very happy. But I can't be sure, She continued. *I have to have proof…*

Then Tara started to wonder. *Why do I have the princess'
name? Another thing, my father's name was also Alek.* She
was about to go into deep thought when she glanced
at her watch. It was late in the evening, so Tara put the
book back on the shelf and headed home. When she
arrived, she put the papers in her lock box and tried to
go to sleep, but the thought wouldn't leave her mind:
why did she have the princess' name?

After breakfast the next morning, Tara went to her
room to change the sheets. She took the sheet off of the
bed, folded it, and then put it away. Then Tara pulled
out one of her mother's old sheets and put it on.

She used to talk with her mother about such mysteries,
like the one weighing on her mind now. Only this is
one her mother could actually provide input on. Oh, if
only she was here now! Tara sank onto the bed and
absentmindedly began smoothing the wrinkles in the
sheet.

When Tara came to the last bump, instead of her hand
flattening it, her hand went right over it. Tara tried
again and again. She tried once more, this time using
her fist, but the wrinkle wouldn't flatten. After a few
more tries, she pulled back the sheet. There was
nothing there.

Tara had an idea. She clipped the sheet to the curtains over her window and then used her hand to feel around the impossible-to-break bump.

Tara soon felt little bumps. She looked closer to where she was touching and found a secret seam. Tara felt around the seam and felt a rectangular shape.

Hmm, She thought. *It seems like there is a pamphlet sewn into the sheet.*

Tara grabbed her scissors and very carefully cut the seam open.

She was right. When Tara was done cutting she pulled out an entry from an old diary.

Tara stared at the book for a while. *Are you meaning to tell me,* she thought, *That my mother sewed this into her sheet? I'm so glad I was concerned about the wash ruining them.* She stared a bit longer, then lay on the bed and began to read.

As she read, everything began to make sense. Starting with the entries her mother made after she got married, she discovered that her father was Prince Alek. Just as she had guessed, he left Persia and married her mother, Rachael, in France.

The Hidden Princess

I suddenly woke up to a large crash as the doors of my nursery gave way to a mob of black-clothed, katana-bearing ninjas.

My father, who had been reading by the fire when I fell asleep, took up his sword and stood between his family and our invaders. "Stay behind me, Martha!" He ordered.

The embroidery my mother had been working on fell forgotten to the floor as she made a quick effort to rescue me from my crib. But one of the ninjas was quicker, springing past my father, taking his katana to my mother's throat, and leaving her to crumple to the floor.

I began to wail while my father, red with distress and anger, slew his wife's attacker. Another ninja made a swipe across my father's chest, creating a diagonal cut in his linen shirt that began to turn red with blood.

My father cried out in pain but continued to fight. When at last it seemed like he was winning, more men streamed through the doorway.

"Get the princess!" One yelled, turning to me. A momentary look of shock overcame his face before dissolving into fury as he yelled, "STOP!"

My faithful nanny—having come in through a hidden entrance in the back of the room—had retrieved me from my crib and was carrying me away. Slipping through hidden doorways and secret passages known only to the palace staff, we were soon beyond reach.

That was thirteen years ago.

Some find it unusual that I remember the event so vividly. It's not like a babe in arms to have such a good memory, but that's just part of who I am. I only need to view something once to have every detail filed away for easy access.

This was an immense blessing to my tutor, who found my schooling to only take the length necessary to read through the material, thus deepening and abbreviating my education. Given our survival status, the less time spent in books, the better.

Even though most of the palace staff joined my nanny and me in our mountain alcove hideaway, I share equally in the hunting, gathering, cooking, and other tasks needed for the sake of food and shelter. You would not recognize me as my parents' heir.

We've done well to replicate a primitive yet functioning version of the life we knew before the attack. Some of the staff even managed to bring palace artifacts: crown jewels, various pots and pans, mattresses, and the pastimes my parents cast aside in their efforts to protect me.

The palace has been left abandoned. While the ninjas did not accomplish their mission, they were the most successful of multiple other parties who attempted to snatch me from the palace. It was too risky to stay.

What makes a child worth so much invasion? The palace staff say a prophecy foretold me to be the key to uniting separate kingdoms. Our neighbors naturally took this as a power statement and were convinced that the kingdom I resided in would outshine the others, so many attempted to steal me away.

They were mistaken and, while we don't know *exactly* what my destiny is, we do know it has nothing to do with politics. I am to be some sort of connector piece between two otherwise divided worlds. When and how this will come about is to be seen.

Nanny is convinced the key is in the last items my parents were attending to, but I can't reconcile that. I remember exactly what Father was reading and Mother was stitching and it had nothing to do with me, a prophecy, kingdom unity, or anything of the sort. Still, it's the only lead I have, so much of the time I've been able to get away from the others has been spent looking over these items.

By this point, I have memorized every one of his annotations and the placement of each of her delicate stitches. They were both brilliant, very good at what they did in areas so starkly different from the other's that they complimented each other wonderfully well. They were like two kingdoms themselves, united by a love that wove them together and overflowed into my birth.

While I have not grown up alone, there is a different kind of loneliness in watching the palace staff raise their children when I have not known the love of my parents outside of my first year. Nanny is the greatest maternal figure I've had, but it's not quite the same when the softness of my mother's cheek and the smell of her hair are just beyond my senses, trapped in my memory.

I remember them holding each other as they watched me in my crib. I remember Father tossing me in the air, to my giggles and Mother's laughter. I remember Mother singing as I drifted off to sleep and my father listened, enchanted. Those were bright days full of love, so much love, yet the connection has been broken.

"'Cuse me, ma'am," a voice shook me from my reverie.

My fingers had paused their tracing of my mother's stitches and I looked from their familiarity to the eyes of our cook. Beyond him was a stranger I did not recognize, an older man with white hair and a thinning beard, dressed in a brown traveler's cloak.

"He says he's traveled a long way to find you," the cook informed me. "He bears your father's signet ring," he added as the traveler stretched out his hand and gave me the object in question.

My heart skipped a beat. How was this possible? My father was wearing his signet ring the night of the attack, but here it was, in as good condition as I last saw it in. "Thank you," I said, nodding toward the cook.

He bowed and left our company.

I turned toward the stranger.

"You've been hiding for a long time, Princess," he said. His voice was warm and friendly, like the loving grandfather I never knew.

"When your adversaries swarm the hills and hunt you down, it is better to stay hidden," I replied.

"They have given up their search," the stranger said, "and besides, you have grown in your acquisition of skills and talents so that you are capable of defending yourself."

"How do you know?" I asked. "Any of that?" I quickly added. We were very particular over the years of when and where we hunted, gathered herbs, and trained. How was he able to watch us so keenly and we not know?

The stranger smiled fondly. "Your father appointed me to watch over you. I have been roaming the land since the attack, throwing your pursuers off your scent and checking in on you every once in a while. Those who trained you were once my pupils, and I didn't let them know all my tricks," he winked.

"But when did my father set you over me?" I asked, eagerness building in my voice.

"Ah, he gave me those instructions when he took your mother from the scene of the attack," the stranger said.

"He survived!?" I asked. "I thought they both perished! But why didn't he come to be with us?"

"Ah," the stranger said. "Your mother was deeply wounded, but not quite killed. He took her deep beneath the palace, where the healing pools lie, a secret oasis of a bunker he had stocked for just such a calamity. It was intended that he would lead any necessary flight there, but the insinuating attack was of such scale and surprise that he was not able to point your nanny in the direction of the entrance. Even if he wasn't on the frontlines of defense, there were too many ninjas to make it to the vault without leading them there. So you and the staff took the secret passageway out, while your father took advantage of a break in the waves of attackers and sealed himself and your mother away where they would be safe and he could heal her."

"But why didn't they come out when our enemies retreated?" I asked. "Or sent for us to join them? We could have smuggled each of us as there was a break in our foes."

The stranger shook his head. "You underestimate how they prowled these lands for you," he said. "You would have given away one hiding spot or another and all would have been killed."

My gaze sank to the floor.

"Furthermore," he said, "as to why they didn't come to you, once the oasis is sealed, you are the key to open it. The three of you were never meant to be separated," he said gravely, bowing his head in remorse. He looked back up at me. "It is only now, all these years later, that it is safe for me to bring you to them."

I took a step forward, eyes locked on him. Could it be true? I get to be with my parents? After all these years? "Show me the way," I said.

A smile came across his face and he turned to lead me from the mountain that had been my hiding place for so long.

Those Three Little Rocks

Irwin was outgoing. He was very athletic and often surrounded by people, but he secretly enjoyed quiet strolls through the park and watching the birds who quickly learned he had a kind hand full of food.

Margaret was quiet. She kept to herself and enjoyed reading books, but her big heart also made her fond of walking the city blocks and greeting the shop owners who knew her by name.

One day she was heading down a busy sidewalk when Irwin missed a step on his way out of a diner and tumbled into her, knocking them both to the ground. The friends coming behind him laughed, but Irwin offered Margaret a hand and a sincere apology.

Straightening and brushing themselves off, the first time their eyes met seemed to slow the world to such a rate that they forgot where they had been going.

After they had been dating for a while, Irwin placed three small rocks, one at a time in Margaret's lap. The first had an "I" on it, the second said "love," and the third "you."

Margaret looked up at Irwin and smiled. She did, too.

Walking through the park one cold evening, Irwin and Margaret leaned into each other's warmth as they passed a street musician and families with young children. Irwin steered them toward a nearby bench where they sat down.

The fairy lights strung through the trees gave their surroundings a magical ambiance. Margaret laid her head on Irwin's shoulder and they admired the way the light reflected off the diamond ring he had slid on her finger a quarter of an hour earlier.

She then slipped her hand into her coat pocket and pulled out the three small rocks he had given her, placing each one in his lap so they read, "I love you."

He looked at her and smiled. "I love you, too," he said.

When Irwin enlisted to fight in the great war happening overseas, Margaret went to the boat docks to see him off. They were to be married as soon as he returned and her heart ached at the separation.

Irwin held her close and slipped those three little rocks into her hands.

She looked up at him, eyes full of tears but a face full of admiration. "I love you, too," she said.

He never did come home.

A young mother puts away her smartphone and takes the hand of her four-year-old son as they continue walking through the grounds of Arlington National Cemetery.

The sky is bright blue and sprinkled with cotton candy-shaped clouds, a soothing contrast to the lush green grass and full trees of early June, but not comfort enough for the ache brought by gravestones as far as the eye can see.

She wants her son to understand that the privileges they enjoy should not be taken for granted. Freedom is not free but bought through the lives of many valiant souls.

Suddenly the little boy breaks their hold and dashes to a headstone just off the walkway. "Mommy, look!" He exclaims. "There are rocks on this one!"

The mother follows her son's path and bends over to get a closer look. "And words on them, too," she tells him.

"What do they say?" The little boy asks.

"I-love-you."

In honor of Irwin Roth (1924 - 1944) - New York City, LTC, US Army

Monica's Metamorphosis

The weather was serene yesterday, as 80-degree weather usually is. There was not a cloud in the sky and a soft breeze occasionally blew, refreshing whoever it touched. Birds happily chirped from their various perches while the sun shone on the earth in a way that felt relaxing whether one stood in the open or in the shade.

To my delight, I had no homework, so I grabbed my favorite book and my hammock and hurried out to the woods behind my house. I have always felt at home amongst the trees, away from the world in a place where I can express my feelings without any negative feedback. In an odd way, the solitude of the woods is comforting.

I hung my hammock in between two trees before climbing in and opening to the first page of my book. Despite having read it multiple times, I was soon fully engrossed in the tale to the point that I did not notice the caterpillar crawling on my shoulder.

The insect's presence did not come to my attention until it reached my neck, where its little legs tickled me. Frightened, my reflexes kicked in and I slapped my neck, which happened to be a deadly blow to the caterpillar. With its last breath, the poor insect bit me before I — now with a sharp pain in my neck — brushed it off.

Since the peaceful mood had been disrupted, I packed up and headed back to my house.

Incidents like this are common in my life, but this particular one quickly became one of a kind. I assumed that there must have been venom of some kind in the caterpillar's bite, which would explain why I felt so terribly sick. The act of reflection soon caused me to realize that I had never before seen a caterpillar like the one that bit me.

By the time dinner rolled around, I had no appetite, so I went straight to bed. However, sleep did not come, so I lay awake in discomfort that only increased as each minute passed. I felt as if my insides were being reworked. And that's when I began to shrink.

At first, I thought I was imagining this change, but there came a point when the distance between my hand and the edge of the bed grew to be undeniably larger than normal. I began to panic. Of all the nights my parents had to choose to go out!

I had never heard of anything like this before. Was I going to shrink into nothing? Then I felt as if something was coming out of my back while my arms and legs began to turn into what looked like a black pipe cleaner. I passed out.

When I went to get out of bed the next morning, I found that—instead of two feet to lower to the floor—I had two wings that lifted me into the air. A rough flight brought me to the bathroom where the mirror told me what I feared:

I had turned into a monarch butterfly.

I continued to stare into the mirror. What was I supposed to do? Was I doomed to be a butterfly forever?

Suddenly my little sister, Skipper, burst into my room. "Monica! Monica! Time to get up!" From the bathroom counter, I saw her realize my absence. "Monica? Where are you?"

By the time I realized Skipper was heading my way, it was too late to hide.

"Monica? Ooh! Butterfly! Come here you pretty little thing!" Skipper grabbed at me but thankfully I was able to fly beyond her reach before she crushed me.

Seeing that I was too far away for her, Skipper ran away yelling, "Mommy! Daddy! There's a butterfly in Monica's bathroom!"

I knew Mom and Dad would let her keep me, so I needed to escape and fast because—with all love—my little sister is not the best caretaker. Life as Skipper's pet would be a short one, to say the least.

Frantically, I looked around for a suddenly needed escape route. I remembered that last night my little sister had opened her window, whose screen she had cut a decent size hole in, so I took off toward her room.

Skipper and my parents caught up with me as I glided into her room, but I flew out the window just in time.

I am in the wild now, but life out here is not so bad. I do miss my family, but I can not live with them in this condition. I do not have to go to school or worry about how I will be able to pay for my future life. No, now my days consist of flowers and long flights through the woods. Now I can live out my days amongst the trees I love so much.

Silence

Marina was a secret agent who specialized in recovering valuable items for people with disabilities. Her fluency in American Sign Language especially helped in the cases of the hearing impaired or a mission where verbal communication could be detrimental. Sometimes Marina was also called in to teach other agents how to communicate with sign language, as it was in a notable case with Felipe.

Some called him sloppy, some called him trigger-happy, but no one could deny that Felipe was excellent at accomplishing the end goal of his missions — regardless of how he got there. He was one to think outside of the box and walk the line between protocol and lawlessness. Somehow he managed to not quite get in trouble, but it was often only a hairline that made the difference.

Marina's impression of Felipe was "flirtatious," an adjective she did not use kindly. From their few passing interactions, she found Felipe to be far too friendly and humorous for such a serious field, so she received her assignment to teach him the language begrudgingly.

Felipe seemed determined to exasperate her. He spent every lesson goofing around, asking silly questions, and not retaining anything she said. If it wasn't required, Marina would have given up on him much sooner, but she stuck to the task. Truthfully, the only reason Felipe even sat in for the lessons was because he wanted to spend more time with her.

Despite all his sarcastic comments and quick remarks, Marina began to sense something deeper in him. He wasn't all fun and games. He was fiercely loyal and confident in his beliefs. Sure, he might crack jokes at anything and everything, but there were definite lines he would not cross, even for the sake of a laugh. Despite what she would consider to be her better judgment, Marina found herself respecting these newly discovered qualities of Felipe, and her sternness — slowly but ever so surely — began to fade.

With each lesson, Marina began to regard Felipe more kindly and he, in return, listened to what she had to say rather than jump at every comedic opportunity. Soon, Marina was horrified to find herself humoring Felipe's weakening efforts to make her laugh. From the indifference with which she began, she now found herself…giggling. She couldn't actually be interested in him. Yet what was definitely her better judgment told her she was, hence her eager willingness to accept an assignment where they were paired together.

They were to retrieve a stolen jewel from an underground labyrinth-like vault. The evil mastermind behind it had spared no expense when it came to setting challenges and deadly traps. Perhaps the riskiest of all was a three-step process with an unknown trigger: (1) an erected barrier that (2) became soundproof 30 seconds before (3) a toxic chemical was released, to the fatality of whoever had been trapped.

They were well on their way to successfully completing their mission when Marina, who was one stride behind Felipe in a long corridor, suddenly ran into a translucent wall that had not been there a split second before.

Felipe stopped in his tracks and turned around, his eyes growing wide with horror. In a frenzy of trial and error, he acted on every thought that crossed his mind and used everything he could find in his many pockets in an effort to set Marina free.

"Felipe, there's nothing you can do!" She cried. "I'm trapped! There's no way out! Please, just—" Marina stopped.

Felipe suddenly seemed unable to understand anything she was saying.

"What?" Marina asked. "What's wrong?"

I can't hear you, Felipe mouthed, holding a hand to his ear and shaking his head. The barrier had become soundproof.

This was it. The last stage. 30 seconds and it would all be over.

Marina's eyes met Felipe's.

He raised his hand. *I love you,* he signed, and Marina wept.

The Perfect Shot

It is evening. The pub is lively and packed with customers who just got off work. Most are good friends and sit in circles around various tables making cheers and having a good laugh. One man sits alone at the bar. He is a gun for hire. Enter a female photographer. She does not know any of the groups so approaches the bar and seats herself next to the man. He looks tired.

PHOTOGRAPHER: Long day?

SNIPER *(snorts)*: More than you know. *(wanting to be polite)* You?

PHOTOGRAPHER *(annoyed)*: Oh, yeah. I kept missing my shots.

SNIPER *(resignation)*: Same here.

PHOTOGRAPHER: Kept cutting their heads off, too.

SNIPER *(amused)*: Yeah, I just do more shooting than decapitating.

PHOTOGRAPHER: Yeah, I'm trying to avoid that.

SNIPER: You just need to steady your shot.

PHOTOGRAPHER: That'd be easier if I had a tripod. Oh, the joys of being a rookie!

SNIPER: So how'd you get into this business?

PHOTOGRAPHER: Oh, you know, it's the only hobby where you can shoot people and cut their heads off without going to jail.

SNIPER: Oh, so you're doing it for the right people.

PHOTOGRAPHER: Best in the business!

SNIPER: Lucky you. Sometimes I'm out in the elements for hours on end.

PHOTOGRAPHER: How often do you shoot?

SNIPER: Oh, that depends. I go out and practice sometimes.

PHOTOGRAPHER: Oh? Where?

SNIPER *(shrugs)*: Fields, mountain tops.

PHOTOGRAPHER: Mm-hmm. I've taken some of my best shots from there, and some of my worst.

SNIPER *(nodding understandably)*: It's all about timing. All you need is to stay focused.

PHOTOGRAPHER: Can I see your equipment?

SNIPER *(hesitant)*: I'm guarded about it.

PHOTOGRAPHER *(whiny)*: Oh, come on! Show me! Look around, *(motions to the circles of distracted patrons)* everybody's busy. No one will see anything.

He guardedly looks around the room.

SNIPER: Alright. Look here— casually.

The PHOTOGRAPHER leans in. The SNIPER pulls back his coat to reveal a pistol in a sling.

SNIPER: Not my biggest one, but ain't she a beauty?

PHOTOGRAPHER *(sits up, dumbstruck)*: I don't think we're talking about the same thing…

The SNIPER looks at her with sudden understanding.

In their moment of realization, one patron glances away from her group and sees the still exposed gun. She screams, sending the pub into a mad scare. Glasses are dropped and chairs knocked over as each customer runs to safety offstage. The PHOTOGRAPHER and SNIPER remain seated, soberly watching the mayhem until they are the last remaining members of the pub and all is quiet again.

PHOTOGRAPHER *(clears throat)*: Well, it was nice meeting you.

SNIPER: Yeah. You, too.

They awkwardly rise and exit in opposite directions.

An Elephant's Tale

Sunlight beamed through the cloudless sky, melting the snow that had been profuse not too long before. Flowers bloomed on the two *árboles* nearby and the family of birds nesting in their branches sang a cheery tune.

Around the trees, two friends played just off from their families, two pink elephants in a herd of gray.

Finishing a round of tag, the two settled in a nearby grove to catch their breath. The surrounding border of tall grass was rustled by a soft breeze and a heron circled a small patch of woods nearby. The two friends watched it silently glide over the trees.

They didn't need to be talking to enjoy each other's company, but they were also fond of entertaining interesting thought lines, as they did now. They had covered every topic under the moon, and she loved that.

"You know," she said, blowing a nearby dandelion, "no matter how long I talk to you, I always leave our conversations with more questions than I came with."

"I guess that's a good thing," he replied, looking thoughtfully to the sky. "It means we'll never run out of things to talk about."

"That's true," she said. "Unless we get mad at each other for some reason."

"I don't see that happening," he said, still looking at the sky.

"Me neither," she replied.

"Just wait," he suddenly added. "Something's going to happen."

She laughed. "That's exactly what I was about to say."

The two continued looking giddily at the sky while—hardly visible on the distant horizon—clouds were beginning to build.

They passed many days in much the same way, slowly but surely becoming fluent in the other's habits and mannerisms so one day she instantly knew when there was trouble within his herd.

Per her inquiry, he talked to her about it. There was nothing she could do about the situation, but it helped him to have a listening ear. He couldn't bear the burden alone and she was able to take some of the weight off his mind.

"Thank you," he later told her, "for being such a good friend."

She smiled but, as soon as they had turned away from each other for the day, she was fighting back tears.

Once safe on the other side of a large bush, she embraced the suddenly overwhelming gratitude until sobs shook her body. *I do not deserve a friend like _him_,* she thought.

The heat of summer was upon them now, strong and undeniable. With it came another reality that the two elephants would soon be ascending the mountain range across the plain. Clouds were building on those distant peaks, but the hike was a rite of passage and their turn was fast approaching.

She looked away from the inevitable future and to the surrounding fireflies. They flickered on and off and back on again, giving the impression of a thousand lights dancing across the dark plain.

The scene was magical, but he could tell her thoughts were elsewhere.

He hooked his trunk in hers, pulling her mind to the present. "You're going to miss this, aren't you?" He asked.

She didn't say anything but looked thoughtfully at their interlocked trunks and slowly nodded. Yes, she was going to miss this very much.

A few days later their conversation returned to their upcoming move across the plain. She put out the idea of claiming the same watering hole, mentioning how a lack of doing so would mean they wouldn't have any connection and therefore might never see each other.

He sensed the fear behind her words and promptly hooked his trunk in hers.

"We are not going to let this separate us," he told her. "I won't let it. Nothing is going to get between us."

Their last night in the place they had known as home was a happy occasion. Many of the elephants gathered to celebrate, dancing hours into the night. That is if one could call their movement "dancing." Their perpetual jumping up and down was shaking the earth more than anything else.

The two friends stepped away from the crazy ruckus of the others to the more quiet outskirts. In the cool grass, they enjoyed dances of their own, leaping and bounding through a time of much fun but one that could not hold back the impending future.

"This is the last time we'll be able to dance together," she told him. The circumstances and limitations of their upcoming journey would not allow it.

"We'll find a way," was all he said.

Soon after, the two elephants set out across the plain, alone in a wide expanse full of creatures they did not know. They wanted to befriend those they met along the way, but there were too many risks and unknown variables. It was easier to depend on the other.

They were resting by a water hole when a nearby dandelion caught her eye. She verbally reflected on the many she had blown during the countless hours they had spent discussing life's many curiosities.

He just laughed. "I hope this works out," he said, "because we have invested a lot."

She couldn't agree more.

There was a bright happiness that came as autumn slipped into place. The surrounding trees and shrubbery were full of the color of changing leaves, teetering on branches until they finally fell into patterns decorating the ground.

The two elephants were over halfway to the mountain range, a change of terrain that—coupled with the change of seasons—formed a low fog on the horizon. The path ahead was becoming hard to see.

He looked at her. "I would consider you to be one of my best friends," he said.

To her, the sentiment seemed out of the blue, but she reciprocated his meaning. Whatever was hard to discern, they knew where they stood.

The closer the two elephants came to the mountain, the clouds they had seen the innocent beginnings of billowed darker and bigger. She began to grow concerned. What if they were caught in a storm? What if they lost each other in it? What if—

"I care about you," he told her.

She looked at him carefully, trying to place his sentiment within their friendship. It didn't seem to quite fit, almost as if he wasn't just a —

A roll of thunder suddenly pulled their attention to the nearby mountain. They could almost see the ascending path, but wind-blown clouds and fog made it easy to lose sight of their trail. They continued forward.

At the foot of the mountain, the two elephants found themselves on the brink of a storm, but they couldn't stop now. They had a summit to reach without delay.

She remained rooted where she stood, looking up the drastic incline to the peak that was slipping out of view. They would be there soon enough, but there was no telling what would happen along the journey. "What if we're not friends then?" She asked him.

"I highly doubt that," he replied.

She gave him a weak but encouraged smile. Their circumstances were maddening, but at least they had each other.

Raindrops began to fall from the dark clouds overhead, each tear-shaped orb contributing to cloudy puddles of stirred-up mud.

A thick fog began to settle around the two elephants and lightning struck the impending mountain.

Melani woke up, the white flash of light leaving her room as quickly as it had entered.

It was raining outside, dreary and foggy. Water was leaking inside through the broken seal of her window, as it did from time to time.

I need to fix that, Melani thought, but she just stared.

On her nightstand stood the figurine of a pink elephant. It was one of a pair, but the other had long since disappeared.

There were many things the start of the day called for her to attend to, but Melani had lost all of her desire and will, so she just lay there and watched it rain.

On a Quest for Something

Maddie opened her eyes.

The first rays of morning light passed through her open window and drawn curtains, softly painting the shadows of raised blinds on her floor and the adjacent bedroom wall where her bookshelf rested.

The bookshelf — a square, nine-compartment construction — displayed the colorful covers of many books, the center block holding a jeweled music box from her grandmother. On top of the shelf was her memory box, the safe holder for childhood relics — nostalgic reminders of in-line skates, wind-blown hair, and hours of imaginative play.

Outside, birds chirped the first notes of their morning song. It was time to start the day. Maddie had to leave for school in 30 minutes, plenty of time to make it through her regular morning routine.

A splash of cold water simultaneously washed her face and woke her up before she brushed her teeth. There was one pimple that must have decided this was a grand day to see the world, but Maddie had a trick for that and moved on to her closet. With the afternoons still being warm, she accommodated for the chilly classrooms by slipping into her favorite pair of jeans, a simple V-neck top, and a light cardigan.

After running a comb through hair that graced her mid back, Maddie straightened the quilt she hadn't moved much in her sleep. Setting up her sleeping pillow and returning two decorative ones made the bed. Slipping her book bag onto one shoulder, Maddie scanned her room for a reminder of anything she might have forgotten. Seeing nothing, she headed to the kitchen.

While cooking the egg and bacon for her regular breakfast sandwich, Maddie heated up one ounce of water and soaked a green tea bag. She then refilled her water bottle and pulled out the wraps she had made for lunch the night before. Pressing the tea bag to her pimple, she waited for the egg and bacon to finish before using her free hand to combine it with a slice of cheddar cheese on an English muffin.

Gathering her belongings, Maddie made a brief pause at her reflection to find that the pimple had lost its puffy red appearance and was practically unnoticeable. Satisfied, she grabbed her keys and headed out where she was immediately struck by the sunrise. Sparing a moment to take in the glorious sight, Maddie let out a deep breath before getting in her car.

Kelsey opened her eyes.

From her nightstand, her phone blared its morning alarm and she made a desperate swipe to silence the ruckus. Her room was dark, shielded by the heavy curtains covering her windows. Comprehension of the time called painful attention to the fact that she had hit snooze too many times. Kelsey's heart dropped.

She threw back the covers and lept from the bed she had only just climbed into a few brief hours before, leaving her comforter and many throw pillows in violent disarray. From a pile of laundry on the floor, she threw on a wrap top and pencil skirt before beginning to fumble through her extensive makeup collection. Thanks to years of practice, she was able to complete a full face in 30 minutes, but even that was cutting it close today.

The bags under her eyes and a growing number of pimples were getting harder to hide, but she had just the trick and reached for a different bottle of cream-colored liquid. It was a nice thought to do some sort of cleansing face mask, but she didn't have time for that right now.

After running a straightener over sticking up sections of her blonde bob, Kelsey resolved to apply her mascara and lipstick at an inevitable stoplight. Securing a necklace from her grandmother in place, Kelsey glanced over her reflection before grabbing the designer bag she'd managed to squeeze her school books into and rushed out the door.

Turning out of her neighborhood, Kelsey's racing mind retraced her frantic steps, double-checking if she had missed anything. She could do without breakfast—just like she'd done without dinner the night before—and one of her friends probably wouldn't eat all of their lunch, so she'd be fine, but she couldn't go one more street without getting a cup of coffee.

With an iced white mocha with vanilla, sweet cream, cold foam, and caramel drizzle in hand, Kelsey was stuck at yet another stoplight. Her eyes darted from the clock to each car that got to whiz along its way while she drummed her fingers against the steering wheel. When one whiz and one drum aligned just right, she realized that—somewhere in her hustle—one of her acrylic nails had snapped in half. Kelsey groaned. She did not need one more thing this morning.

Maddie had been settled in her seat sketching for 20 minutes when Kelsey rushed into the crowded lecture hall just as the bell rang. Someone had taken her seat. Frantically looking around, Kelsey headed for the first empty spot she saw and slipped down beside Maddie.

Kelsey let out a deep breath and Maddie glanced over at her, wide-eyed. Kelsey seemed tense, high-strung, and

unable to relax. Maddie then noticed the teacher
approaching his lectern and began putting away her
sketchbook.

Maddie did not understand how someone could live as
Kelsey apparently did. Surely they would burn out or
mentally split from so much stress and no relief. What did
she do for quiet reflection? Did she have any at all? How
could she live without it?

If anything, Maddie probably spent too much time in
thought. She was keen to pick up something artistic or just
space out at a wall— processing, reflecting, and considering
how things may turn out in the future. How did Kelsey
keep track of everything a college student was responsible
for, let alone do it well, if she was always running from one
thing to the next?

"Good morning, class," the teacher called. "Please put
everything away for a pop quiz."

The sound Kelsey made was like a punctured balloon
releasing the last of its air.

———————

Most students silently packed up a few minutes before the
bell, trying to slip their belongings subtly into their bags,
but the sound of their zippers gave them away. When the
bell finally rang, the room was therefore quickly emptied of
everyone except for Maddie and Kelsey, who had been

taking notes all the way up until dismissal. They each jotted down their last word and then began packing up.

"How are you coming with the project?" Maddie asked.

Kelsey's eyes grew big, remembering one more thing she had to do. "I've read the instructions," she replied. "And looked over the rubric. I have a few ideas but I'm really now sure which one to pick."

We only have one week, Maddie thought to herself. "Maybe we could work on it together," she said. "I'd appreciate another perspective on mine."

Kelsey met her eyes and gave a smile of relief. "That'd be great," she said.

Maddie smiled back and they headed out the door.

"Ohh," Maddie sighed, practically melting as she stretched her arms out in the sunshine. "I didn't realize how cold it was in there," she said.

"I'm warm-blooded," Kelsey said as they headed down the sidewalk.

Maddie crossed her arms in an effort to warm her cold fingers. "When does it begin feeling cold to you?" She asked.

Kelsey shrugged. "November," she replied. "Maybe December."

"Wow," Maddie said. "I start shivering sometime in October."

"What's your favorite season?" Kelsey asked.

They came upon a trash can, which Kelsey dropped her coffee into. It was more water than coffee at this point, but still, Maddie did not like to see things wasted.

"Um, fall," Maddie replied, looking at the trash can until they passed by. "You?"

"Summer," Kelsey replied.

"The heat of summer or the activities of summer?" Maddie asked.

"Oh definitely the activities," Kelsey replied. "But more so because I get to share them with my family."

"Really?" Maddie asked. That was something she could relate to.

"Yeah," Kelsey replied. "My grandma's house is on a lake, so we spend a lot of our summer there. Sometimes I go up during the year just to be somewhere quiet."

Maddie's gaze was fixed on Kelsey. "Why would you want to be somewhere quiet?" She asked.

Kelsey looked to her left. "Oh, a couple of different situations I just need the mental space to think about," Kelsey said.

A group of boys passed the opposite way just then. Kelsey glanced at them and then kept her gaze fixed on the ground in front of her.

Maddie looked from the group of boys back at Kelsey.

"Do you ever wish you could go back and change one thing you really regret?" Kelsey asked.

Maddie slowed in thought, her mind suddenly flooded with images and memories from a pain recently passed. They came to a pause where another sidewalk branched off from their path.

"Yeah," Maddie replied, "Though I find I would have never become who I am today if it weren't for that experience. So no, I wouldn't go back and change anything. I'm in a good place now, and though it was hard and long to get here, it was worth it."

Kelsey studied Maddie's face until another passing group of students led them to step a little more out of the way.

"You'll get there," Maddied reassured her. "It may be raining now, but it can't last forever."

Kelsey nodded, coming back to the present. "Thanks," she said.

Maddie let out a deep breath and looked around. The trees around them were changing colors and the birds were singing. It was beautiful. She looked back at Kelsey. "My class is this way," she said, gesturing down the sidewalk that branched off from their initial path.

"Mine's over there," Kelsey said, motioning the opposite way.

"Well, let me know where you're free to work on that project," Maddie said, stepping onto her path.

"Yeah," Kelsey said, turning as well. "Let me check what else I need to do and I'll get back to you."

"Sounds good," Maddie replied. "See ya later!"

"Bye," Kelsey said, and they headed on, each intrigued that someone they had seen one way for so long turned out to have a lot in common.

The Simple Life

At eight years old, she was the ringleader of the neighborhood children. Thin and with uncombed hair that dipped below her lower back, she was a head or two taller than the rest. Each of them, with distinct tan lines from many hours at the community pool, was marching barefoot into another day of exploring the woods surrounding their homes.

They filled their time with many games of make-believe, traveling to time periods long past or seeing more in their surroundings than was actually there. Adjacent trees became homes, a grocery store, a city hall, and a post office, forming a town that each of the children took on a role to maintain.

In the cul-de-sac, one could find chalk-marked traffic patterns for the bikes, rollerblades, scooters, and go-karts parked on the side. The surrounding trees were full of leaves and birdsong, their strong shadows occasionally distorted by the passing of cotton candy-shaped clouds. One could hear the sound of a distant lawnmower. In the backyard, a garden full of snap peas, strawberries, cucumbers, and blueberries was enjoyed for playtime snacks.

Toward the end of another activity-filled day, colorful pool towels could be found hanging over the back porch railing to dry. Long shadows gave light to a firefly-speckled yard and stacks of plates sparkled in the dishwasher, freshly clean from a favorite meal. Pattering feet in just-adorned bathrobes line up at the counter for smoothies and butter toast. Stacks of books waited for them upstairs, one last journey to a far-off place before sleep finally overcame them.

At 18, she was wrapping up her high school experience. The last four years had not been easy, but she had grown close to three girls she would hold onto for the rest of her life. She went to school dances where her outdoorsy nature gained a refined grace. Volunteer activities were profuse on her calendar and she began work at a local mom-and-pop shop.

She seemed to always be running around, from one activity to the next, but her favorite times were the unscheduled evenings when she was home to share dinner with her family. If no one had pressing matters to attend to, they often spent hours around the dining room table, eating at first, then continuing to talk and play games.

Other times she and her sister would curl on top of her bed and color, her open windows letting a soft spring breeze play with the curtains. Candlelight and a symphony of crickets led each to take a deep breath and enjoy the moment at hand. No matter where they could run off to or what they could possibly fill their time with, a checklist of completed projects could not compare to the value of quality time with the people who mean the most to you.

She was 22 when she made his acquaintance. He did not catch her eye at first, and getting to know him was not the roller coaster she had read romance to be. It wasn't falling at all but rather like finally getting to truly know an old friend, taking one step at a time and somehow just knowing that each one was heading in the right direction.

It was wondering and then hoping she would see him again. It was wanting to have another conversation, share another laugh, and then wishing she didn't have to say goodbye. It was wanting to share an experience with him when he wasn't there and choosing to experience whatever with him when he was. It was the immeasurable comfort and ease she suddenly found his company to bring her.

And then it was learning just how messed up he was and choosing to love him anyway. It was simultaneously letting him in on the qualities she pretended not to possess and receiving that same cultivating love in return. Then it was a total disregard for anything that could be gained and realizing she wanted to give him what she could give *because she could* give.

He followed a similar line until one day when individual growth, community approval, and time aligned. He took her to a quiet place only they knew and asked if she would take on life with him for however long they had left to live. She agreed absolutely.

She was 26 when they had settled into a quaint house right down the road from where they grew up. Heavily involved in the community they had invested their youth in, they spent much of their time pouring into others. What time they had at home was spent building a world of their own, forever working together on one project or another.

They were standing back to admire the completion of their latest renovation when she let him know another pair of hands would soon be joining their team. He just stared at her, trying to comprehend the meaning of her words, but the realization that finally dawned across his face was her pride and joy.

It was quite a strange feeling to be carrying another life, but it was a state that made her glow with a deeper-set happiness than any she had felt before. She hummed about her work more than usual, enjoying the process of swelling so large that things had to be done differently. It was fear, joy, anticipation, longing, and love.

And then she was holding that new life in her arms. A smile that glowed, eyes that sparkled, and a laugh that filled one's soul with happiness. It was like holding a light and, even when that light seemed to be giving nothing but rain, she couldn't help but envelop it with love.

At 30, she had three children four and under, each with a wild imagination and bright-eyed curiosity. It was the age when everything was new and undiscovered. They had lots of questions that their parents loved to discuss with them, each conversation laying a brick in the starting foundation of a lifetime of learning.

They were a troop, the five of them, marching off for another day of work and play as time and capacities differed. Bed sheets hung to dry doubled as laundry and a great ship out at sea. Dishes were a wonderful matching game. Weeding entailed a lesser but still important role in a greater tale. There was a balance between work and play that made seemingly mundane tasks have the potential for so much more.

But her favorite thing was reading them bedtime stories, tucking them in only for covers to be hastily removed in a flurry to point out the story they would like to hear. She had read every book on the shelf to them, from the simplest to the most complex. They were eager to learn the code of letters themselves, and she taught them all they could take in, but for now, found joy in the plots they wanted to hear again and again (and again).

At 40, her oldest was fourteen and tasks looked a little different around the home. Outdoor exploration had been an independent feat for many years now, so dinner time entailed accounts of far-off places and many adventures. They took every minute—and made many more—to hear about everything each individual had experienced.

Questions and discussion still reigned but had grown in depth as each child began to take on the weightier matters of friendships and finding one's place in the world. Laughter was no stranger at their table, but they also shared many tears and worked through several differences. There were not always joyous sentiments between each other but the underlying love of their familial bond was never questioned and immediately defended if threatened.

They cultivated an atmosphere of trust and growth, hard work and harder play. Everyone had a place and knew they had a purpose. Whether prepping food, serving in their community, or the constant resetting of chores, everyone was needed yet knew they were loved for much more than their work. They had space to discover their own unique gifting and a support system to help navigate.

This led to a quieter turn in the once boisterous pastimes. After-dinner gatherings became a scene for instruments and singing or individual entertainment such as quilting, reading, sketching, or jigsaw puzzles. In the warm cool of summer evenings, they enjoyed such activities on their back porch. In the winter, they bundled up to the soft crackle of their living room fireplace, but it was the company of each other that made their time enjoyable.

At 50, the children were marrying and their home began to return to how it was in the beginning, albeit with wrinkles of experience around their smiles. It was like getting to know each other again in a whole new light.

They woke up with the sun each morning and again worked directly with each other throughout the day. They reinvested in their community, plugging in where wisdom began to outbound what they could offer in agility. She got in the habit of writing lengthy letters to friends and family and reading to him in the evening, a cup of tea in hand and another glorious sunset on the horizon.

By the time she was in her 70s, they had formed nonverbal communication so synchronous they didn't even need to look to know the other's stance. Many grandchildren had joined their number and she took up crocheting to make them each a blanket of their favorite color. Yarn and hook in hand, she spent much time working in contemplative peace by an open window. Beyond, a pleasant breeze rustled leaf-laden branches and children happily played.

She was 90 now and sitting alone in the backyard where they had seen so much life. The sod they had spread as a young family, the garden where many hot days were endured to yield lush produce, the cool summer evenings they spent enjoying the fruits of their labor. The yard was trimmed and up-kept, a soothing contrast to the trees that had once again grown wild and full on the other side of the fence.

Above their lofty tips, she could see the glory of the sunset, reflecting shades of orange, yellow, pink, and purple on the smattering of clouds that sailed slowly by. Through the trees, golden beams of light danced between new leaves.

She almost would have called it magic and watched it as long as it was there to behold.

She wondered what he was looking at now. What kinds of other-worldly riches were beyond the extent of her imagination but in the realm of his? She wished she were with him to share the sight, but she would be there soon enough. It was almost time now.

One by one the chorus of birdsong faded into a symphony of crickets. At each reflection the yard was darker than before, growing dimmer and harder to make out. The dance of sunlight and leaves had faded into a warm glow that sank lower and lower until, at last, the sun slipped to the other side of the horizon, revealing the garden of stars.

Like a Fairy Tale

It was a quiet neighborhood. The streets were shaded by ancient trees and paralleled by up-kept sidewalks. The houses beyond were unified by their standard mailboxes but otherwise completely unique. One had yellow siding, a tidy white picket fence, and flower beds full of marigolds. Another had chosen pastel purple and deep green shrubbery. On and on they went so you couldn't quite pick one out from the next. Yet, in the cool of this summer evening, number 456 was distinguished by two couples sitting on the front porch while two young children played in the side yard.

The house belonged to the boy and his parents, who had invited the girl and her parents over for the dinner they had finished half an hour earlier. Now the four adults sipped sweet tea and mixed the quiet of the evening with conversation.

The fathers looked off into the distance, much farther than their eyes would betray, into the distant past they shared and the uncertainty of a future they didn't know if they would see. While the mothers minded things of the present and watched their children from afar, even they couldn't see what might as well have been reality for the little boy and his new companion.

They had finished a round of tag and collapsed in the soft green grass, laughing. Sitting up, they caught their breath and looked back at the house. It was made of red bricks with rich green shingles. The front porch railings were white and draped with oversized flower boxes that looked out to the half-crescent driveway, at the center of which there was a fish pond with a small waterfall.

"This might look like an ordinary home," the little boy told the girl, "but for those who have the eyes to see, it is so much more."

"What do you mean?" She asked, looking back at the house. Sure, it wasn't like any home she had seen before, but it was just a house.

"Look at the flower boxes," he directed.

She did. "They're overflowing with strawberries," she observed.

"Yes," the boy confirmed, "I would say ridiculously so, but why? Look closer." The little girl focussed her attention, squinting slightly until she caught the flitter of a small body passing between the vines. The girl gasped. It was a fairy! But it wasn't alone. In fact, there were dozens of fairies moving throughout the plants, replenishing the berries that had been picked that afternoon. Yet, in their excitement for the season, the fairies kept tripping over the vines, haphazardly spilling a little too much growing dust on one berry or another so the fruit exceeded its standard parameters and swelled into shapes that more so resembled fans and planets.

The little girl stared in awe and the boy smiled. "That's not all," he told her, and she looked around to find that what had seemed like an ordinary yard only moments before was now teeming with magical life.

There was a mermaid sitting alongside the fish pond and trolls standing guard at the front of the driveway. One had just finished its rotation and was returning to their underground dwelling. A griffin flew overhead and she followed its flight until she caught sight of a friendly giant passing in between the trees, whose branches were laughing in the wind.

"They listen to all your stories," the boy told her, "the trees. They take in all your memories and play them back when you need to remember. I see mine sometimes, running in between the trunks."

The little girl looked at the trees very closely, convinced she saw one wink at her "Is your house just as…?" The little girl tried to ask, unable to find the words.

"Oh, yes," the boy confirmed. "Did you not see the ghosts that joined us for dinner?" The little girl shook her head. "Is that how…?"

The boy heartily nodded. "Mom's cup got knocked over and the food seemed to disappear a little too quickly. They were enjoying themselves just as much as we were, perhaps even more so," the boy added. "And there's an invisible person in the garage that keeps walking away with Dad's things. We've spent SO much time trying to uncover his hiding places."

The little girl laughed. "What else is there?" She asked, her eyes dancing with wonder.

"Oh, lots of things," the boy replied. "Hidden entrances to secret rooms in the closets, an underground village in the basement, a seaside getaway in the bathroom. There's even a lonely black hole in the attic. I go up there often and tell it all about the outside world, at a safe distance, of course. It takes everything in."

"Maybe I could meet it, too," the little girl said, completely missing the boy's joke.

The boy looked at her thoughtfully. "It would like that," he said, looking back at the house. "You're different from the kinds of visitors we're accustomed to."

"Like who?" The little girl asked, amazed there could be more.

"Oh, we've seen them all," the boy said. "The house is more like a depot, a one-stop shop for dwarves, orcs, elves, pirates, and world travelers to buy and trade goods of all kinds. They tell stories of great feats and heroic adventures, the exotic and the unbelievable. You never know what you're going to get."

The little girl blinked. She didn't know how she hadn't seen it all before, but now that she had, she couldn't look away from the entire world the little boy had helped her see.

A Songbird's Summer

Co-Authored by Nathan Janowski

The songbird loved the summer weather in her hills just off the mountains, but winter was coming like a parent telling their child what they will do next. The songbird knew she would have to leave her trees and the wind that carried her through their branches because the weather would be too harsh for her hollow bones. She would have to fly south, across a great expanse of land and then a great expanse of sea to a small group of islands where she could wait out the winter snows.

The first of the trees had not started putting on their fall color, and the songbird had yet to see a migrating flock, but she was not one to wait for others to begin before she was to start. There was too much to do in preparation for fall. Besides, she did not need someone to follow. She could make the way just fine on her own. It would be time to leave soon enough, so she set out to make the most of the days she had left.

While the songbird's preparation for winter was simply to fly away, her friends had much more work lined up. A mother bear and her four cubs, a ferret, a hedgehog and her son, a family of rabbits — all had stores to fill and beds to make, and food to eat for the months ahead, and the songbird helped in any way she could.

For the bears, she scouted caves. For the ferret, she investigated burrowing ground. She gathered beetles, caterpillars, and earthworms for the hedgehogs and grass, straw, and twigs to insulate the rabbits' den.

Back and forth she flew, all day and late into the night, carrying this or that for those she couldn't leave without helping as much as she was able.

"You do too much," a white-tailed deer commented on the songbird's flight.

Preparation for winter was at its peak, so the little bird only paused long enough to hear the deer out.

"You need to learn to say no," the deer said.

"Oh, no," the songbird trilled. "This is my treat. I find no greater joy than knowing my friends can benefit from my measly efforts."

The white-tailed deer was not convinced, but the little songbird continued on. She was unwilling to waste a moment among the creatures and places she'd given so much time to, and redoubled her efforts to do all she could before she had to leave. Twig, beetle, den. Burrow, earthworm, straw.

Little by little, winter's preparation fell into place, and the seasons began to change.

———————

The songbird dodged a falling leaf and dropped one last twig into its place atop a beaver's dam, just another little project she found she could help with.

She came to a rest on a branch overhanging the bank near the grateful beaver, and the two admired their work. A soft breeze blew by, carrying a slight chill that erased the songbird's smile and made the beaver shiver.

"Where is it that you're going again?" The beaver asked his small friend.

"The islands down south," the songbird replied, staring blankly at the beaver's lodge.

"Oo, very nice!" The beaver exclaimed. "I would love to go with you."

"You and everyone else," the songbird replied with a sigh, recalling similar comments made by all the others she had helped. "That's the difference between you and me," she said, blinking and shifting her gaze to the bank below. "You *want* to go. I *have* to go."

"But there are so many reasons to want to go," the beaver replied. "The places you'll see, the things you'll get to do."

"I'd rather if you could go," the songbird said. "With all you do to maintain the river, you deserve to enjoy a place like the islands."

"You do, too," the beaver said.

"Maybe," the songbird replied, "but I'd rather stay here, in this place with those I love the most."

The beaver did not have a response, and the two eventually parted.

The day for her to leave came like a final warning. She could wait no longer, she could do no more. So in the dark of early morning, long before the rest of the hills were awake, the little songbird left her summer nest and headed out over familiar territory for the last time that season, paying keen attention to every detail and hoping she would see it again.

Too soon, she reached the river bordering her homeland from the wilderness beyond. With a heavy heart, she let the wind carry her wings over the coarse waters and then blow away the tear that slipped from her eye. There was no turning back now. Only forward.

The dawn that found her hours later seemed to fill everything but the songbird's spirit with sunlight and happiness. Surely great things did lie ahead, but all she could think about was what she was leaving behind and the markers she would have to reach before she could return.

Land, ocean, island, ocean, land, she repeated to herself. *Land, ocean, island, ocean, land.* It really wasn't that much. She would be home soon enough.

She flew over miles and miles of trees, fields, valleys, and mountains, but the songbird did not look away from the horizon to try and find enjoyment in them. There was no time. She could only stop to find a meal and a safe place to tuck under her wing for what sleep might come, then off again.

Day after day she flew until, at last, she reached the ocean. It would take one day to cross the expanse of water, so the songbird stopped on the shore to rest and gather food.

The songbird was exploring the surf when she came across other animals finishing their last preparations for winter, though a quick acknowledgment was all the time she spared for them.

I can't stop to talk now, she thought. *There's no point.* She would leave this beach tomorrow and never see these creatures again. Why take the time to invest in them if she would not see the fruit of her labor?

While she was quick to move on, the other creatures reminded her of the friends she had left behind. Many of them would work without ceasing right up to the first snow. Why couldn't she stay to help? Why couldn't she give them her wings so they could see the world beyond their hills? She was so accustomed to flight and going, but the others could only dream.

Having filled her stomach and found a sheltered place to sleep, the songbird settled for the night, feeling remarkably resentful of the weather, her wings, and her inability to change her circumstances.

She woke up while it was still dark and—before it was even light enough to see properly—was winnowing her way far above the ocean alongside many other birds who filled the sky around her. They were all headed to the same group of islands, but not all for the same reason. Some traveled the whole world, crossing oceans and continents yearly.

Ducks, grabs, and cormorants gave a full display of their colors and patterns as they flew. Other land birds like doves, woodpeckers, and cuckoos kept their heads on a swivel, trying to see everything and talk to everyone all at once. Still larger birds—namely the cranes, loons, and storks—had to be ever so careful with their huge wingspan so, firstly, their strokes wouldn't capsize the small birds, but also so everyone would take note of how swiftly they could progress.

The songbird didn't fit in with any of them. She just wanted to get to the islands and return home as quickly as winter would pass, none of this show-and-tell that filled the air with a cacophony of noise— noise she knew would ring ceaselessly throughout the islands all winter long.

The songbird fixed her gaze on the horizon and tuned out the garbled chatter. *Maybe I should fly over and join their camaraderie,* she thought, *make acquaintances with those I'm on this journey with.*

She glanced over at a cockatoo laughing too hard to fly straight.

No, she decided, looking back at the horizon, *there will be plenty of time for that later. Winter won't end sooner if I start the formalities early.* One little stroke at a time, and she was a small way closer to those she ached to see again.

"Taking advantage of the slipstream and knocked the company, I see," a voice called from behind the songbird.

Looking around, she found an albatross gliding just above her flight path. He coasted to her side and then gave one sweep to not fall below. There was no way to miss the large volume of air that he had shifted.

Compensating for the change, she answered him, "With the amount of air you move, any bird would be wise not to fly too close."

"But you're not flying with any birds," the albatross pointed out. "You're alone, flying your course. Did you leave all your friends behind to fly south?"

"I would have given them my wings if I could," the songbird replied, "but they have their own responsibilities to carry out and the ability to do so through the coming cold. I do not, so I am flying alone."

"Then make some new friends," the albatross said, as if this was the most obvious thing in the world.

The songbird laughed, unconvinced.

The albatross continued, unperturbed. "For the little I know of you, you left your friends for the winter as you had to. They will go on living their life, and you must live yours. So why are you only taking advantage of the safety and protection of a flock," he said, nodding to all the other birds, "and not their company? Make some new friends."

The songbird didn't respond. *What does this "ocean spanner" know?* She thought. *You can't just make a new friend. It takes time to talk and listen, to allow open communication and build trust that grows into a friendship. I'll be flying home before I could even begin that with these birds.*

"I've been flying over oceans my entire life," the albatross said, interrupting her thoughts, "and while I'm fully capable of doing it for the rest of my life, choosing to be alone when there is company to be had is a waste."

The songbird considered his words. He was right about that much, at least.

"Conversation with others can remind you of the beauty you've grown accustomed to," the albatross said, "and help you see the world differently. You're not cheapening the places and friends you left behind when you engage a new friend. Your friends will still be there when you return, but how would it be if you didn't have anything to tell them?"

"I don't want to talk about me," the songbird immediately replied. "I want to hear about their winter, the laughs *they* shared, the lessons *they* learned, not jabber ceaselessly about my own."

"I have found that if you want someone to share about their experience, you also need to share about your own," the albatross said.

The songbird opened her beak, but the retort she desired was not found. He was right. Friendship was supposed to be mutual giving and receiving, not one party doing all the talking and the other doing all the listening.

"I have all winter to learn new things from the other birds," she finally said, her gaze fixed on the horizon, "if there's something to learn at all. I have made this journey countless times before without much difference between trips. I doubt this one will have anything new to tell."

The albatross gave the songbird a quizzical expression, then went back to looking ahead. They flew along in silence for a time.

———————

By the time the sun was high in the sky, the great cacophony of talk from the flock of birds had decreased to a low chatter. The focus of every bird was on the next beat of their wings.

With miles of ocean on every side, the songbird wished the waves were treetops, that there was solid land under her so she could rest when she wanted. If she could be in her own hills there would be no worries about direction, conserving energy, wind change, storms, or wondering if she should get to know strangers.

She had met other birds before. They had shared the airways, their experience on the islands, and stories of the storms they had gone through. She hadn't seen any of them since. The world was so big, full of so many birds going from one place to the next. The songbird was lost in all the rush and busyness, lost in the endless sky full of strangers.

I don't need something else to do as I try to keep my head about me on the islands, she thought.

Food wasn't a concern for the visiting flocks. The island trees were bursting with fruit, nuts, and insects. The jungle also provided plenty of shelters and, if worse came to worst, you could always find cover among the human shelters. Some of the buildings even had enough space for the larger birds and there was plenty of fish around the island for those carnivores in this migration.

At this thought, the songbird looked around for the albatross. She was going to ask if he ate meat, but the first thing she noticed was dark clouds. What she had taken as the beginnings of nightfall, she now recognized as miles of thunderheads towering high and ominously in the path of their migration.

The birds began to fall into formation, flock with like flock.

The geese moved into their V-formation, the starlings swarmed together, and the swifts made a boomerang shape— each tight wedge meant to handle the turbulent weather ahead.

The songbird looked around for birds of her kind but found herself quite alone. She had just decided to stick close to the flock of geese—thinking she would have the best chance of cover from the rain if she flew under them when the storm broke—when all the migrating birds suddenly flew straight into sheets of rain.

The songbird was blinded by the torrent of heavy raindrops. She tried to make it to the geese but they had already disappeared. All she could see was the dark sky above and the black sea below.

Crash! The lighting sounded like the fall of a great tree but a hundred times louder. Every raindrop caught its light so, for a moment, the songbird's world looked like a silver forest. Then she was plunged back into the pitch-black storm.

She desperately tried to keep level, knowing that if she dropped in altitude she would be taken by a wave pushed up by the wind. But the songbird was battered down by rain, with no idea of direction and no way to see other birds.

All at once, the rain stopped coming from above her. There was still plenty of wind and the horizontal rain you find in these kinds of storms, but she had flown into some kind of shelter. *There is no shelter this many miles away from land,* she thought, and realized that there must be a larger bird above her, blocking most of the rain. *Well I'm not going to lose this piece of good fortune,* the songbird thought.

The next time lightning lit up the storm, the songbird could see a white bird with a wingspan so large that she couldn't look from end to end in the split second. She also couldn't make her voice heard over the wind, so she focussed on flying, conserving as much energy as possible for the unknown distance left.

The first sign that the storm was breaking up came when the other birds became visible through the rain, though only when lightning flashed for it was well dark now. The sky was competing with the sea for the title of darkest mass.

The songbird didn't know when the light from the human buildings started to show through the storm, but there they were: small dots of light splayed out in front of her. Close, much closer than she would have thought.

She could see the illuminated shapes of those tall buildings and the lights of the smaller dwellings. She made for them eagerly, her exhausted wings putting in the last effort to bring her to safety.

At one point she realized she had lost her cover. The other bird must have flown on, deeper into the island. For a moment she had the thought that she would never be able to thank the bird for the cover, but then she flitted under a porch roof and out of the steady rain. Landing on a joist holding a ceiling fan, she knew she had made it to the island full of winter migrant birds.

The songbird woke with a shake and the sights, sounds,

and smells of the human world pressing in on her fuzzy mind and tired body.

The porch she had landed on turned out to be an apartment balcony someone had added rafters to for effect. From there, the songbird could see many variations of other apartment buildings. The standard was beige or cream with variation coming from plain or colored apartment doors and items that lay about in the walkways or on the roof.

The streets at the feet of these buildings were alive with the endless soundtrack of music, air compression from stopping buses, foot traffic, car horns, cheers, and hollers. Not to mention bird chirping, airplanes passing overhead, and boat horns from the bay. Occasionally it all would be overcome by the sirens of emergency vehicles.

If she tried, beyond all those noises the songbird could hear the ocean: visible beyond the buildings in distinct shades of blue. A clear tint speckled with swimmers and surfers stretched farther than one would think right before suddenly dropping to a dark blue shade speckled with sailboats, cruise boats, and cargo ships of all shapes and sizes. She could see a little of the thin beach lining the city-filled coast before it gave way to a mountain sitting between two bays.

Further still, tall buildings turned into homes that seemed like brown and salmon-colored rocks squared away in every inch of unclaimed land. Then they broke into fingers that stretched up mountains paralleling the coast. Dark clouds and rainstorms hovered there but seemed to stay away from the sunny shore.

A breeze engulfed all of this — soft in some places, strong in others, but consistently colder than the songbird expected, sending intermittent shivers down her spine.

A broody pigeon suddenly flew into the songbird's line of sight. The creature was fluttering in and out of overhangs, hopping along rooftops, and examining nooks and crannies for any secure spot protected from the elements — very clearly in need of a nest without delay.

"Excuse me, ma'am!" The songbird cried out from her spot as the pigeon got closer. "This perch would serve your purposes well I think."

"No, no," the pigeon cried back. "That's too close to any human eyes. They would break up the nest when they notice it. That won't do."

"I understand," the songbird trilled back, "but there's a spot here in the rafters that's obscured from any prying eyes."

The pigeon promptly flapped over to look. "Oh, yes!" She exclaimed. "And look, there's even a back way out of this crevice under the roof, between the rafters. Well, this will have to do. I just hope that these humans don't come out here to smoke or yell at passersby. I would hate it oh so much if my babies saw that kind of behavior. How fortunate it is that some bird left feathers behind. Those will do very well for the nest. Now I must get twigs and sticks…"

Seeing that the broody pigeon was having a hard enough time flying her own weight around, the songbird decided to help her build a nest. She had made plenty for herself and used a similar technique to help her friends in the hills, so she didn't think it would take much time at all. It was plenty of time, however, for the pigeon to tell all about her flight over the ocean, how she got separated from her partner, and how the lack of humidity made the smallest of differences when flying.

"But you know," the pigeon trilled as she dropped another twig into their collected pile, "it's the smallest things that make the most difference."

The songbird tied off a portion of the nest and picked up her next twig.

Once the pigeon got through talking about the different types of twigs and which ones fit together the best, the songbird had a chance to ask about the pigeon's mate. "How do you expect your husband to find you on the island?"

"Oh I expect he'll have no trouble with that," the pigeon replied. "I won't be hiding from him, you know. Us birds do form quite a tight-knit group. Give it a few days of morning song and I expect that he'll find me."

"But you don't even know if he made it to the island," the songbird had to say. She wished nothing but the best for the soon-to-be mother, but it was no uncommon thing for birds to not make it.

"Well that's true, my dear," the pigeon replied, " but I have no doubt that we'll be just fine. I mean, isn't this the proof of it? You didn't know me from a flock this morning and now you've helped me ever so much with the nest and been the best of company. Oh!" She suddenly exclaimed. "I do feel something coming on. I must situate these feathers. Thank you again for showing me those wonderful yellow fruits earlier."

"The pleasure has all been mine," the songbird replied, bobbing her head before she hopped out from under the shelter into the joys of a job well done.

As she flew, however, the pigeon's words began to bother her. *The best of company…* The songbird repeated to herself. She thought back to her friends in the hills, to the conversations she enjoyed as food was being gathered, and the long evenings when both conversationalists were tired. But the mere exertion of that energizing community had breathed life into her tired wings, unlike now.

No, the songbird thought, *I'm not very good company right now, and that's okay. Creatures are naturally grateful for the help and I'm glad I was able to lend a wing where I could.*

The songbird found that she had flown out of the bustling city and down a long road where the cacophony of noises faded into silence. On the inland side towered dome-like mountains covered in green grass. Dark gray rock peeped out here and there and trees lined each outermost crest. They looked like turtles or sleeping giants that at any moment could get up and walk away.

Where human habitation disappeared altogether, there were mountains of severe lines, jagged ridges folded one after the other like creased paper. The grass growing on top was of a green so bright it looked unnatural. The songbird flew lower and found that her aerial view didn't capture the majesty of looking up at such heights from the road.

All those stone giants stood tall as they faced the sea, where teal-colored waves caught the afternoon light before crashing onto beds of rock. The water spilled into bowls and pools of all shapes and sizes as it returned to the sea. Again and again, a dark blue bump thinned into a teal curl before foaming white and leaping many feet into the air upon contact with the shore.

The songbird came to rest on a wide bar of sand just before the rocky beds. The sun reflecting off the beach was blinding, but it felt good to rest her wings, so the songbird squinted and tried to take in the beauty around her.

This is where they wanted to be, the songbird thought, thinking of her friends in the hills as she looked from the mountains to the sea and back. *The beaver, the ferret, the bears — They all wished to be exactly where your toes are right now. Enjoy it for them.*

But she didn't. She wanted to be back home doing the work that kept them busy throughout the seasons, not flitting around all winter eating and enjoying the scenery. She didn't get it. Why did she have to leave? Why couldn't her hollow bones be thick enough to last the winter in her hills?

The islands were overrated, she concluded. Sure, the native creatures lived here just like those in the hills lived there, but these airways were swarming with migratory birds "oohing" and "ahhing" over every little thing as if they'd never seen it before.

The songbird looked down at the sand. It was coarse and polluted with yellow and black specs. She gathered some under her feet, then released and smoothed it out as best she could.

I don't want to be remembered for the places I've migrated to, she thought. *I don't want to be known for interacting with creatures from all over the world.* She wanted to be a small yet essential part of an effort that would reach beyond her wingspan and benefit someone other than herself— kind of hard when those she found she was able to help were land and sea away from her.

The beaver wanted to be here, the songbird thought, looking up at her surroundings again. She should be grateful for where she was at, the opportunities she had, but all she was doing was whining and complaining. She didn't deserve to be here, not when she stood in the place of those with much better attitudes.

Maybe it was just from squinting too hard, but the songbird lost a tear that fell to the shore and absorbed into the sand. How could she be crying in a place of such supposed beauty? The songbird shook her head and flew to a fence post between the beach and the side of the road.

The sun was low in the sky now, bathing the shore in an orange light. There was a mixed group of birds further down from where she had been. They were giddy with activity — gathering island flowers, collecting shells, eating fish, playing in the sand.

Do they not all have homes they're longing to return to? The songbird thought. *Friends they're missing terribly?*

"Wow! Look at that sunset!" A lark suddenly exclaimed. "It's beautiful!"

The songbird looked down the shore and saw the many colors fading daylight had turned the clouds, but she couldn't tell what made them beautiful.

In a grove of fruit trees, two owls were searching for food. The couple seemed to be newly formed as they had that timid vigor about themselves that a new thing commonly has as it learns its place in the world. The owls flew from one branch to the next enjoying the breeze at the top of the trees, then the shade at the bottom, talking to each other as they went. Occasionally, the female would pick a fruit and then call her mate over to have a taste.

There were plenty of other birds around, going here and there talking and singing. The noise was endless, the sound of the ocean always a deep undertone.

The songbird couldn't say why she stuck around, but with nowhere to go and no interest in flying at the moment, she found herself and the owls to be constant features. Eventually the owls noticed this as well.

"Do you know what the sun's doing to the land west of us?" This question came from the male owl. He had landed on a branch just in her line of sight.

"Excuse me?" The songbird asked, surprised and thoroughly confused.

"Hello," said the male owl. "My mate and I are rufous owls and I was wondering why you look lost."

The songbird was taken up short, her mind still trying to figure out the first thing the owl had said to her.

Before she could find the right words, the female owl came over to tell off her husband. "Leave the poor bird alone, dear," she said. "You shouldn't spring that kind of question on just anyone."

"It's no trouble," the songbird interjected. "I've stayed here as long as I have because there's no particular place I need to go, but I'm not entirely sure what you meant by your first question."

"Oh don't mind that," the female owl said. "My man studies the sky and how it changes."

The male owl spoke up at this point. "My first question referred to the curvature of the earth and how creatures would see the sun differently at the same time."

This intrigued the songbird, though she still wasn't quite sure what he meant.

The female owl sighed. "Darling, that's all well and good, but do you really think that was the best way to introduce yourself?"

"No trouble there," chimed the songbird. "I like things that make me think and I don't have much use for small talk. I much prefer to go straight to the things that make you, you."

"Or what makes who, who," the female owl said.

They all started laughing.

Over the course of the afternoon, the songbird learned that the two owls were the perfect blend of corny jokes, absurd questions delivered with a serious face, humility for things they didn't know, and all-around good cheer.

When the songbird learned that the owls were flying on to another part of the island, she ensured she asked about the odd question that had instigated the fun afternoon.

"Oh, well imagine that there's three birds miles and miles apart along the equator," the male owl said, "so far apart that the sun is in a different part of the sky for each of them. Now if the sun is setting on the first bird in this line, and the sun is directly overhead of the second bird, then the sun would be rising for the third bird. It's sundown, high noon, and morning at different places all at the same time."

"And the sun blesses them all equally," the female added. "Wherever you are on this planet, we are blessed with a beautiful opportunity called *now*."

This gave the songbird pause, but before she finished fully hearing what was said, the owls' were saying their goodbyes and winging their way across the sky.

"You're right," the songbird said to the empty space, feeling anew the absence of friends.

How could that happen? The songbird thought, catching the title she had just involuntarily given her companions. *I didn't — I couldn't —* All the excuses she had given the albatross flew back into her thoughts. But what had just happened? She had made friends.

No, that's not quite right, the songbird stubbornly thought. They had made her a friend. The owls had pursued her, invited her into their conversations. Yet something deep inside her had called them "friends" without hesitation. Was this what the albatross was talking about? Is this what he was trying to encourage her to do?

The songbird sighed and tried to find enjoyment in the sights and sounds around her, she was just not interested.

In another aimless flight, the songbird came across a part of the island that had been decimated by a long past volcanic eruption, leaving the entire area covered in nothing but rocks. Brown rocks, black rocks, gray rocks — rocks, with a road winding throughout.

The black rocks were smooth and shiny. They looked like large scales with how major cracks ran this way and that. The gray rocks were a plethora of chunks, piling up into little mounds for goats to traverse. The brown rocks lay on more fertile ground, occasionally giving way to an odd-looking tree or — at times — being completely spotted over with large puffs of dried field grass.

On and on the rock beds rolled, as far as the songbird could see until she found herself suddenly beholding clouds arched like a rainbow as they stretched inland from the sea. A second look caused her to realize that—at some indistinguishable point—the rolling rock beds took a treeless slope up into a mountain that could be mistaken for sky.

Where is the horizon? The songbird wondered. The land seemed to roam on and on here.

She continued her course until she spotted a patch of green grass. It had to have been planted and maintained by humans, given the amount of human dwellings around it, but there were trees that the songbird recognized.

She gave a little chirp and flew into one particularly tall, particularly green tree. The leaves were full and soft, just like back home. She found a nook in the tree and nestled in.

A soft breeze blew through the branches and the songbird could hear leaves rustling. A happy trill escaped her beak and she ruffled her feathers contentedly.

On her way back from a coastal flight, the songbird noticed a large white bird roosting in one of the trees in the area she'd found. It wasn't doing anything particular, in fact, it looked half asleep, but she thought she recognized him.

She landed opposite the albatross and looked him over. He looked fully fed and well groomed, so why wasn't he out seeing the island and making new friends out of strangers?

The songbird shook out her feathers and nestled onto the branch to sit for a time.

Just as the warmth from the sun started to put the songbird to sleep, the albatross shook out his feathers and stretched his wings wide. Blinking as he took in the world, his gaze came to rest on the songbird, who at that moment was trying to wake herself up by shaking her head back and forth.

"It's good to see that you've fully recovered from the storm," the albatross said. "It surprised me when you disappeared through the rain heading toward the city lights."

"You saw that?" The songbird asked. "How long were you flying where I couldn't see you?"

The albatross shrugged. "I was never too far from you the whole way," he said. "I wanted to talk to you more about how you were going to spend your time on the island."

The songbird chirped in surprise and annoyance. "Well what about you?" She asked. "I expected you to be off not giving anyone a moment of quiet, trying to make everyone your friend."

"Oh is that so?" The albatross chuckled.

The songbird didn't know why she was being short. She knew better than the pointed words she had said.

"So how have you found the island?" The albatross asked. "As beautiful and full of life as ever?"

The songbird resigned herself to this question. "It's as it's always been," she replied, picking at the bark just in front of her. "Nothing new. Just as full of noise and birds as always. Nothing's changed."

The albatross looked at her intensely, leaning forward on his branch.

"What?" The songbird chirped. What did he want from her? "The islands are as beautiful as always," she said. "The flocks of birds can't get enough of the sights, the beaches, the mountains, the shells. They go on and on about how everything looks so beautiful, so different from wherever they're from."

The songbird could have gone on, getting more emotional as she went, but the albatross interrupted her momentum. "How have you been missing your friends?"

The songbird felt that right through her little bird heart. *No!* She thought. It was hard enough trying not to think about all the things she was missing. She was not going to try and explain herself to a bird she barely knew.

"What do you want me to say?" She finally asked. "That I've made new friends? That I've collected some beautiful memories to share when I return home?"

The albatross looked at the songbird for a long minute. When he did speak, it was in a melancholy, almost sad voice. "I don't know who told you that you had to spend your days on the island busy and going, but that really isn't the point of any of this."

There was a long pause before he continued. "I really don't know anything about you, so I hope this will help, but — Well, I'll leave the 'but' for later." The albatross started over, "I think you're missing the purpose of winter, of migration. You've become so focused on what it's taken from you, there's been no place for thinking about what it's given. You have to get your beak out of your own way, reason with your presumption on how the world works, notice what no one else notices, ask what is beautiful about what's in front of you, and then listen and see what the world will give. You'll meet so many creatures who will tell you things that you never thought of. Let yourself open up to that possibility and it will nourish you in a way you never knew you were missing."

The songbird thought of the owls and how her pretenses dropped as soon as she was caught off guard by an intriguing question.

The albatross continued talking. "When we first met, you dismissed the islands because you didn't see any purpose in them, in coming all this way with nothing to do but wait for winter to be over. You were seeking a purpose, any purpose to keep you occupied. But because you were wholly focused on purpose, you missed the opportunity for community. You need both. I don't think you would disagree."

The songbird shifted her gaze to a different branch.

"With all that being said," the albatross continued, "you miss your home, your friends, and that's okay. But you're here by no choice of your own. You've been taken out of where you're comfortable and where you know what's what. I would tell you that it's so you can go back singing louder than ever," the albatross said. "Use this time to rest, think, spread your wings— knowing that it doesn't really matter how. You'll go back to your friends in the hills, but if you don't gain anything from this, what was the purpose? Is the world really going to take everything from you and you not get as much out of it as possible?"

The songbird looked at the albatross to find that he had a wry smile. She stood as tall as she could. "Well since you've had your rest, you're obviously in a talkative mood. Are you ready to get as much out of this day as you can?"

The albatross threw back his head and cawed at the sky. "It would be my pleasure."

It had rained sometime the night before, hence all the puddles the songbird was flitting about in now. She was flying nowhere in particular, just unable to sit still.

She didn't quite know what to do with everything the albatross had said. His monologue was a complete whap upside the beak, yet she felt so seen and heard. For not knowing anything about her, he had accurately laid out the complexities she'd been turning over all season. He was right, so incredibly right, and she was going to be reflecting on his points for a while.

The sound of someone collapsing caused the songbird to look around.

Her flight had brought her to the foot of the coastline mountain and, on a nearby rock, she saw a crane limp from overexertion.

The songbird flew over. "Can I help you?" She asked.

The crane's eyes were wide and it was breathing rapidly.

"Water," the songbird realized. "You need water. I'll be right back."

As fast as her small wings could carry her, the songbird whizzed back to the closest puddle she had seen. Plucking a leaf from a nearby bush and holding both ends in her beak, the songbird scooped up some water and flew it back to the crane. Carefully, she poured the contents of her pouch into the crane's parted beak and rushed off to collect more.

Puddle after puddle the songbird flew, bringing as much liquid as she could back to the crane. At last, the bird began to revive and sat up a little.

The songbird set her last collection of water in the shade of a nearby shrub and helped the crane over to it. Settled out of the sun, the birds caught their breath.

"Thank you," the crane whispered, getting her tongue back in working order. She had a thick accent. "I should have taken water breaks, but I was so set on getting back to the base of the mountain."

"Why didn't you fly?" The songbird asked.

The crane gave a weak laugh. "The challenge, I suppose," she said.

The songbird gazed off. She could relate to that.

"You're from the hills?" The crane asked.

The songbird looked back at her. "Yeah," she said. "The hills just off the mountains. You?"

"The flat plains and gently rolling hills," the crane said. "I'm at the end of my migration and will be flying home soon."

The songbird looked at the crane with intrigue. She had never met someone so far from her home.

"I've heard so much about your area," the crane said with similar interest. "I'm even learning your birdsong to better equip my migrations. Convenient, yeah?" The crane chuckled, nodding back to the rock where she'd been lying limp shortly before.

"You're doing very well!" The songbird encouraged, impressed. "You have an accent, but I would never know you're studying."

And with that, the two fell into seamless conversation. They compared their different regions, discussing the environment of their home, region-specific food, and the specific customs in their areas. The crane asked the songbird about idioms her studies didn't cover and the songbird reveled in the exercise that made her think of familiar things differently.

The songbird didn't know cranes from the flat plains could be so friendly, granted she had never interacted with one personally before. The crane was equally encouraged, saying the songbird's friendliness and openness to conversation was what she loved about birds from the hills.

The two chirped for a while under that shrub, then all the way back along the coast 'till the crane's path deterred back to its flock.

The songbird found herself singing sometime later as she glided through the evening air. She was just off from the mountain that blended with the horizon when a twirl toward the coast dwindled her flight to a hover.

Before her, a golden scene of light painted rolling rock beds and clouds alike in yellows, oranges, blues, and purples. With the sea in front of her, the subtle mountain to her right, and entirely surrounded by a rugged panorama — it was the kind of landscape the humans took time to capture with paint and brush.

She looked around for someone to share the view with but found herself alone. *I could try to describe it to the albatross if I see him again,* the songbird thought as she continued to flap in place. But really, nothing but presence could take in the sheer majesty of it.

———————

The songbird was following a gentle breeze when she found herself gliding over soft slopes of black, ground-up volcanic rock.

It was evening, but only the soft lighting might have given that away with the overcast skies. It was cool. Rain was coming from the clouds, but it was light enough to be a refreshing mist rather than a pesky drizzle. The songbird didn't see anyone else as she followed a path that led between sinkholes and then began descending into a skeletal forest.

The ground continued to be black, the rocks were black, and then the trees also proved to be black— all charred from some long past catastrophe. Yet from their desolate state sprung new life: grass, ferns, leaves— so fresh and green they almost seemed to have a neon glow.

The songbird couldn't take her eyes off the striking contrast between light and dark, death and life, black and green, and took in each variation. A small fern peeped out from under a rock, green leaves sprung from black trunks and charred branches. How could so much beauty come from so much disaster?

The ground below leveled to a forest floor and the songbird glided into a spacious, skeletal wood. The trees were taller here, stunted from their growth yet continuing on. Their leaves were oval, bright green, and had sweltering red boils piled one on top of the other.

The forest began to thicken as the songbird made her way across the landscape. Tree by tree, she flew into a tropical rainforest growing along the rim of a crater. Terrain that could've been looked over for quite some length a moment before was now limited. Trees, fallen palm branches, and plants with abnormally large leaves kept the songbird's sight nearby.

She stopped and hovered where she was at, looking from ground to sky and at the surrounding vegetation. There was something soothing about a forest that made seclusion in one comforting rather than frightening.

On and on she flew, but was this really a flight? Catching the soft breeze that came through the trees meant she was gliding more than she needed to flap her wings. Maybe this was what flying could be like if she enjoyed the scenery instead of trying to get to her next destination. It was about the journey anyway, wasn't it? What there was to learn and see along the way rather than victorious completion.

Then she came to the edge of the crater and glided down into its walls. The diameter seemed to extend forever and made the songbird feel like an ant in comparison. The bottom of the basin looked like stirred water, only it was rough and made of solid rock.

Halfway across, the incredible rockiness smoothed out, aside from the wide fault line of broken volcanic rock — equally fallen in and sticking out. It looked as if some large serpent had sped along just below the smooth surface, leaving an unmistakably broken trail above that led across the basin to a steam vent beyond.

At the center of the crater, the songbird was struck by silence, actual silence. For the first time all winter, she could hear the wind because it was whistling by, not brushing against something else. She looked back at the rim she had come from. Trees lined the edge and, somewhere in them, there was the distant chirping of birds. It was quiet. So incredibly quiet. No hustle, no rush, no chaos. Just the utter stillness and presence of the moment.

Maybe I should continue on, the songbird thought, but where else on these islands full of noise would she be able to hear her thoughts undisturbed and release the defenses she had been holding up? *I'll stay a little longer,* she concluded, *soak it up while I can.*

The songbird took one long inhale, and then one deep exhale that undid knots and released tension that had been squirming in her stomach for weeks. Nothing to take in, nothing to process, nothing to filter, nothing to guard. Peace.

———————————

The songbird was sitting in a low tree across from a waterfall, watching other creatures and human tourists alike come and go, each standing in awe of the scene before them. Yet her eye was drawn to a little fern just off to her left. She was fascinated by its color and shape. The songbird stared at it, again wondering what was wrong with her.

How can I find so much beauty in a small plant and miss the grandeur of a waterfall? She wondered. Why couldn't she also stand in awe of the bigger picture like she did with the forests in her hills?

Suddenly the albatross' words sank in, and the songbird realized that she'd had an upside-down view of migration.

The songbird hung her head and looked at the bark beneath her claws. She had been letting herself think more and more that she didn't ask for the inability to spend winter in her hills, that migration was somewhat of a waste, and how much more involved she could be with her woodland friends if she did not have to leave for a season.

Okay, yeah, the songbird thought, *but I didn't ask for what I've considered to be blessings either.* Who was she to say one thing was bad and another was good? *Migration is a gift,* she thought. *It has shaped and influenced me far more than I realize.* That was not something to be dismissed but a blessing to celebrate and use for the sake of another.

―――――――――

In the cool of early morning, the songbird set off for one last flight around the island before it was time to turn home for the season.

She took a slow glide just above a shaded path carved by humans and covered in rocks, leaves, and roots encased by dust or mud. Up, down, and around the cliff face it wove, each bend giving sight of a slightly more visible coastline beyond and below, slowly regaining its color from the black of night.

At last, the trail was broken by a bubbling river, dancing around and over dark rocks covered in rich green moss. The songbird sailed across and into a pine forest on the opposite bank, where she greeted a cardinal and his son with her cheery morning song.

Through the trees, she could see the beach further downstream and wove through the trees until she came upon a bed of large, egg-shaped rocks. The collection spanned the length of the cliff-lined beach, gradually becoming boulders as they neared the sand until all ceased at the flat and shallow continuation of the river, whose crystal mountain waters had taken a sharp left turn and continued lengthwise down the beach.

The songbird crossed this part of the river and glided the opposite way across the golden sand until she reached a pool at the river's bend.

She landed on a rock nestled in the side of the pool. Across from her, a small waterfall replenished the area, laughing with joy at the opportunity to ceaselessly dive without condition.

Other gray rocks rested at the bottom of the pool, adorned with patches of moss and complemented by waves of sand decorating the riverbed in intricate detail. Tadpoles and small translucent fish looked up at her curiously but didn't dare to get any closer.

The songbird continued to gaze at the water until a trick of light caught her eye. She blinked and looked closer. The sunlight that had just crested the ridge above was catching in the water and forming stars that danced across the bottom of the pool. The songbird cocked her head. *How can that be?* She wondered. The bubbles caused circular shadows, the ripples created mirroring lines, but these star-shaped spots of light seemed to come and go with no natural explanation.

The songbird looked around with changed eyes, taking in every detail as if seeing the world for the first time. The dark gray rocks, the golden beach, the rich green tree-covered mountains, the jewel-tone blue of the ocean. Land and sea, sky and earth, mountains and ocean, rivers and rocks, sand and dirt. It was balance and color and life and beauty unlike any she had seen before.

The songbird was trying to look harder, open her eyes wider, soak in more, but it was all so blissfully overwhelming and too much to grasp, so she took flight once more to explore.

Heading back down the shore, the songbird looked again at how the river followed the length of the beach. *It could have cut straight across to join the ocean,* she thought. *That would have been a lot more efficient.* Instead, the river rippled along the longest way possible. *Where does it go?* The songbird wondered.

Down the cliff-encased shore she soared until she came to the end and found an alcove in the cliff face, undoubtedly the home of many in centuries past. The river continued around the corner and into a shallow opening in the cliff face, just tall enough to fly through without touching the water.

Inside, the cave ceiling escalated to a height far above any human head, and the water flowed right through to an equally as large exit, splitting around a brief sand bar in the cave's heart.

Leaving the cave, the ceiling had sand-colored streaks in its stone gray, marking currents of old. Around and out the water flowed, back into the sun where it was bordered by a clean curb of golden sand. Two large rocks marked where the mountain water finally met the ocean.

To her left, the shoreline continued in an infinite ribbon, golden sand repeatedly met by the pure white sea foam lining rich blue water. This part of the coastline was still blanketed in shadow from the dark gray cliffs covered in rich green trees that towered straight and high above.

It was too beautiful for pride or cynicism to intentionally taint and undid any of the songbird's remaining efforts to keep to herself. Gliding free and unbound in the ocean breeze, the songbird looked down the infinite shoreline. She did not know where it went or what it held, but she was open to the joys and challenges that came from hard yet beautiful things.

As soon as the songbird got in her trees, she was welcomed by the light and the breeze.

For Cami, the Australian couple, the Hispanic couple, Josh and Shyanne, Harry and Mouse, and above all, Nathan — for helping me see the trees through the forest.

194

On the Road to Tomorrow

The path was long and snaked through a plain that seemed to stretch forever on each side. It was a well-worn path littered with rocks that caused its travelers to stumble. They all tripped or stubbed their toe at some point or another, and they all knew the darkness they were walking away from, but not all knew where they were going—especially one traveler who wandered alone.

He was a short-sighted kid who was dressed in rags and didn't have any shoes. The darkness had been all he had known. It was a swell that had no shape or form, like fog with water molecules or night in the middle of day. The traveler knew he had to get out, but he didn't know where to go or how to get there. Happening to stumble across the rock-littered path was the alternative direction he came across, so he headed out.

With each step, the short-sighted kid found his surroundings getting brighter and brighter. He progressively squinted more until he was beyond the swell of darkness and could do no better than keep his eyes on the ground just beyond his feet.

As his eyes adjusted, his vision became better, but he was still hindered by his short-sightedness. He could tell the path led to a bright place, but he couldn't make out the details. To him, it was just a big white blur filled with gold, orange, and copper-colored blobs. Behind, he had progressed so far that he could make out the mass of darkness he had left. It reached high into the sky and seemed to stretch endlessly to the right and to the left.

The boy's heart quickened its pace. The darkness was repulsive, yet alluring. He wanted to stay away, but felt like he was being drawn. Or maybe the darkness was moving toward him. The boy took a step back, then turned around and continued on toward the great white blur. He had to keep moving, he had to stay away, he had to— The boy looked back, and promptly tripped over a rock in the path.

"Ow!" He exclaimed, applying pressure to the wounded member before dislodging the rock and tossing it aside. "All of you are being no help at all," he said to the rest of the surrounding rocks sticking up from the dirt.

If they had faces, they would have been staring back blankly.

The short-sighted kid huffed under his breath and proceeded to loosen each offending object, tossing it to the side of the path. Pushing past the little cuts each rough edge embedded into his hands, he continued up the path loosening stone, after stone, after stone, again, and again, and again, tossing it aside one after the other after the other.

It was a monotonous, tedious, mundane job— so the short-sighted kid was surprised to find satisfaction in his work. Despite the cuts, he had done something to the path, cleaned it up, made it easier to use—even had small piles beginning to form alongside the path—and that felt good.

Good. Yes, it felt *good*. That was a new feeling to the boy, one he had not experienced in the darkness that—

He looked back again. The darkness still seemed to be creeping closer. Why wouldn't it stay put? Why couldn't his progress put permanent space between himself and the thing he wished to leave behind? Why was it—

The backward step the boy took right then landed him on a particularly jagged rock that sliced open the arch of his foot.

"Argh!" The boy exclaimed, falling to the ground and pressing his wound. Lifting his hand a moment later revealed blood. Sniffing back the pain, he tore off a piece of his clothing and tied a bandage in place.

He sat there for a while, contemplating why he was trying to progress and where the path was actually taking him and if he'd ever be able to leave the darkness behind him. He didn't know, he really didn't know, so he just loosened another rock and tossed it beside the path.

A thin line of blood surfaced where the rock broke the skin of his finger. The short-sighted kid just looked down at it before turning to the darkness. It wanted him, and something in him wanted it, but the swell had already taken so much that could not be replaced. He wouldn't go back. He wouldn't.

Several more rocks were shaken from their place and tossed aside before the boy stood with new cuts yet newfound resolution. He turned toward the great white blur and continued up the path. One step at a time, the next one would be better. The next one would be better. And to his surprise, it was— incredibly wonderful and absolutely overwhelming in the most blissful way. So he kept walking forward, one step at a time, not knowing where he was going but discerning that something wonderful lay beyond. He just had to get there, away from—

He looked back at the darkness. It seemed to be following him. He continued forward, then looked back again. He paused and squinted. It really did seem to be getting closer. No, he wouldn't let it. He would outpace it. And the short-sighted kid turned around so promptly he stubbed his toe.

"Mmgh!" He huffed, stooping to loosen the offending object and toss it aside, wincing, before taking care of several others in spite of the small cuts they entailed. He had to stop doing that, but the rocks kept popping up when he least expected them.

The boy let out a deep breath and continued forward again. The next step would be better, the next step would be better. So on he went toward the great white blur of golden blobs.

He had gone quite a ways when he caught up with a shady blur that turned out to be another traveler, a blind girl. She was dressed in colorful yet faded pieces of fabric and had a walking stick to help feel out the path before her. She had paused that slow monotonous job between two boulders hugging the path to learn the coming of the traveler she could hear behind.

As the boy approached her, he saw that some of her "color" did not come from bright fabrics but wounds that had crusted over from where she had fallen. An old gash on her arm, a faded scar on her face, and new blood trickled down from where she had landed on her leg.

"Your leg, it's bleeding," he said, reaching toward her. "Let me help you."

"Oh, it's nothing," she replied.

"No," he insisted. "You may be too numb to feel it, but it'd be best to stop the flow."

The blind girl stared blankly ahead. "Okay," she finally said and loosened a scrap of her own clothing.

The short-sighted kid knelt down and began dressing her wound.

They shared about their journeys as he worked. The short-sighted kid learned that she was also making her way to the great white blur, yet she spoke about it with such feeling, he would have been sure she had been there before.

The short-sighted kid tied off her makeshift bandage and looked up at her, cocking his head slightly. "How come your eyes are significantly worse off, yet you can see so much farther than me?" He asked

The blind girl leaned against one of the boulders. "You don't need eyes to see what I can," she replied as he sank onto the earth beside her. "It all comes from a heart that believes."

The short-sighted kid gazed at the ground. "I want to believe," he said.

"But you're afraid," she discerned.

The boy looked at her. "Yeah," he said.

The blind girl nodded, her face giving the empathy her eyes could not portray. "You want to run free into the possibility of such a future, but you're afraid the darkness will find you there."

The boy's gaze was back at the ground, mentally recollecting what he knew lay behind him. "How can I since there's a swell of darkness within me attracting the darkness behind me? It's going to find me and convolute any reality I could put myself in."

"Only if you let it," the blind girl replied. "But as you know the shape and location of the matter, you know exactly how to keep it out of your future."

The boy looked at her without answer.

"How do you keep running into the rocks?" She asked.

The boy gazed off. "I don't see them when I look away from the path to the darkness behind."

"Exactly," the blind girl replied. "You must keep your focus on the path before you and the place you're heading."

"But I don't even know what that is," the boy replied, looking over her shoulder at the gold, orange, and copper-colored blobs.

"You can't know," the blind girl replied. "That's why we're on this path: to find out."

They continued on in such a way, she envisioning the future beyond and he clearing her path of — and guiding her around—the rocks. She kept his mind off the darkness behind by engaging him in conversation, and he helped her "see" by detailing the world her eyes could not take in on their own.

Every once in a while, he would glance back at the darkness and she would get too caught up in what lay beyond, and both would trip and fall, but they were able to help the other get back up and re-focus on the task at hand.

As the journey continued, such instances became less frequent as the path went from being rocky, jagged, and rough to smooth with tufts of grass growing in popularity. At length, as they stepped onto a grassy knoll, it became evident that they had stepped just inside the border of the great white blur. The ambiguity was beginning to come into focus, yet perhaps even more astonishing was the change they saw in themselves.

"Your clothes!" The short-sighted kid exclaimed. "They look brand new!"

"Yours, too," the blind girl half-whispered.

The short-sighted kid looked down at himself in delight. Even his cuts and wounds had healed, just the slightest silver trace of where they had— He suddenly looked back up at the blind girl. "I didn't tell you that," he said.

Her eyes were no longer glazed over but bright and brimming with tears. "I can see," she hardly managed to get out.

Joy overcame the boy's expression. He looked to where they had come from and found the fading scenery crisp with clarity he had not known before. The mass of darkness was a long way behind and he could see now that it wasn't moving toward him after all. He could also make out the form of a group of travelers who were soon passing by as they headed further into the great white blur.

"I heard the path was going to be a lot more difficult than that," one member of the group told another.

"Yeah," the other agreed. "I think they were talking about the rocks, but most of them were cleared away."

"Yes," the third member confirmed, "and the piles they made up along the path were a comfort to me that we were still heading in the right direction."

The first two nodded in agreement as they left earshot of the boy and his companion.

The no-longer-blind girl looked at him, smiling and shaking her head. "And you thought it all had no meaning or purpose," she said.

The boy shrugged, but he too had a smile that was slipping past his defenses.

They turned then, once and for all leaving the path and the darkness behind, and continued on to learn the reality of the gold, orange, and copper-colored blobs.

Behind the Stories

Princess Fiona

All writers have to begin somewhere. For me, it was at eight years old with this cheesy, undeveloped tale of a princess and her friends. This is my oldest piece of work, and while it could be taken to much farther places, there is a simple innocence to its original form that sets the first stepping stone in the maturing of my writing that the subsequent stories unfold.

A Little Girl's Story

I grew up believing no one understood me, so this short story came from another effort to communicate what was weighing heavy on my heart. It originally ended with the return of the firefly, but my high school career and college experience added new sections I could have never foreseen. From a simple allegory about happiness and lost friendship, God wrote a theme about contentment and what one really needs in life. It isn't about what you've lost or opportunities you've missed but what you still have today and Who has been sustaining you all along.

Lauren's Royal Life

I had a lot of *American Girl* magazines on hand during my elementary school years, many of which contributed clippings to illustrate a story I had written for my younger neighbor, Lauren. With a pencil and the large, clumsy handwriting of a child, I wrote enough to fill the Winne the

Pooh notebook I chose as my vessel. Beginning in 2009, I was satisfied with the story and my revisions by September 30, 2010. Naturally, it didn't take too many more years for my perspective to fall far away from "done." So back to writing I went with this story that I envisioned to be the first of a five-book series. Brainstorming became the extent of that vision as the increasing weight of my academic load hardly allowed more than a few paragraphs to appear on the pages of books two and five. Now this initiating tale has been left unexpanded to reside as a short story.

Nature Royalty

This story steps into the make-believe game that filled many afternoons growing up. From Halloween makeup and dress-up to running around the woods behind our house— my sister, our neighbors, and I embraced the idea of being royalty in the great outdoors. The rules were simple: all the girls were named after plants, all the boys were named after animals, and the boys had a solemn duty to guard their designated princess at all times. The game was more so just an opportunity for us girls to get dressed up, but the band of us shared many laughs we still treasure today.

Adah

At the end of my seventh-grade year, I participated in a week-long drama camp that put on a play about the Biblical story of Shadrach, Meshach, and Abednego. I was cast as a walk-on, my absolute favorite role as I was able to enjoy the production process without the pressure of memorizing lines. I had three appearances: first as a Babylonian captive being taken from her homeland, second as a wine bearer at the king's feast, and third as a witness to the fiery furnace scene. While I was a nameless background figure, I took the details I did have and embraced the role with the full force of my imagination. From Hebrew names to the sandals I contributed to my costume, I created a world behind my character to inform my facial expressions and how tightly I gripped those cast as my husband and daughter (which was a little too tight, I was told). I wrote the first section shortly after that week and added the second two sections after college.

The Mysterious Figure

On the last day of my first semester in the eighth grade, a few new friends and I instituted a book club— not one that gathers to read books, one that gathers to write books. We dreamed of collaborating on multiple projects, beginning with the first chapter of a story that came to Abbie. It was about a girl disguised as a boy who comes across as a mysterious figure to the main character, whose barista parents secretly work for an agency. Abbie intended the story to be about a secret war, but my then untamed leadership strength grabbed hands with a newfound love for Janette Oke's *When Calls the Heart* and changed the genre to romance. When I finally realized that re-dressing another's story is not a way to write, change in the seasons of life led me to put down the story that had become my project. I seriously revisited the composition shortly after college and realized, by severing the sections I had so grotesquely tried to propagate, I had another story to add to the collection in this book.

The Kidnapped Princess

This short story was initially meant to be the cap of a book series that began with an elongated version of "Lauren's Royal Life." Each of the originally envisioned five books would tell of the next royal in Lauren's line. "The Kidnapped Princess" was intended to be a mystery novel unpacking how the ancestry was lost and Tara's discovery that she's a princess. This series finale was never finished, but what I did get down was enough to be something of a short story.

The Hidden Princess

I have no idea where this story came from. It is so unlike anything I'd written prior. I was thirteen at the time, which is when my siblings and I were in our *Ninjago* phase, so my best guess is that I had a pen nearby when a random thought line about a raided nursery occurred. I also remember that it was only the beginning. I had no vision for how the story would end. In the following years, the text bounced from file storage place to file storage place. I added a little here and there but didn't sit down with it again until after I graduated from college. Drawing blanks from there, I turned to some friends to help me brainstorm where the stranger in the brown cloak would take the story.

Those Three Little Rocks

The summer before my sophomore year of high school, my family took a two-month road trip throughout the northeastern United States. One of our many stops was Arlington National Cemetery in Washington D.C. I had never seen so many gravestones in my life, so I suppose it's no surprise my eye caught on one that had three rocks sitting in a line across the top. The marker, attributed to Irwin Roth (1924 - 1944), was a stride or two off the road so, for the sake of not walking on the grass, I did not investigate. My curiosity and imagination, however, spun a possible story into existence.

Monica's Metamorphosis

The English II class I took during my sophomore year of high school spent a unit or so studying novellas, *The Metamorphosis* by Franz Kafka in particular. As an exercise, we had to adapt the story by writing an essay of our own. With minor edits, this is the story I submitted. And you can tell this was during me and my siblings' *Barbie Life in the Dreamhouse* phase because I was inspired to name the younger sister Skipper.

Silence

I was hopelessly romantic and morbid as a child, which entailed the creation of a lot of death scenes. At one point, I had a collection of many ways I could be fatally wounded — each of which ended with my childhood sweetheart arriving just in time to hear my last words (typically "I love you") and hold me as I took my last breath. This story is a more refined bi-product of that incredibly cringy, immensely cheesy phase.

The Perfect Shot

During my senior year of high school, I took Introduction to Theatre to fulfill my art requirement. Of the many things we studied and did in that class, one was playwriting — which naturally entailed us writing a small script of our own. I had no idea what to make mine about, so I simply wove together the many puns that were coming out of my image-heavy roles on the newspaper and yearbook staff. As I am not one to send a crowd rolling, this story is a bit of a stretch for my ability to tell a joke, but it made me laugh when I found it deep in Google Drive during the compilation of this collection.

An Elephant's Tale

This story is the export of a broken heart trying to make sense of a friendship that — by seemingly all measures — never should have ended. Of the many things that hurt, the biggest one I couldn't reconcile was a list of previously said statements that sharply juxtaposed actions I was suddenly receiving. Our friendship felt like a dream. *Did that really happen?* I wondered. *Did we really say that? Were we really that close? What happened?* Out of my perplexion came this story about a dream I once lived and Melani waking up to the reality I was facing at the time.

On a Quest for Something

Similarities and differences have always been something that intrigued me. Being homeschooled up until high school, such observations between the lifestyle I was used to and all those I was meeting had a strong presence throughout the rest of my academic career. It wasn't until my last few semesters of college — when I got to know a girl with whom I had the same such differences — that I truly saw how surface-level differences do not take away from things we all wrestle with. You can connect on a number of deep topics with someone who has a different routine and preferences than you. Turns out we're not quite that different after all.

The Simple Life

Personal grievances with how complicated life can sometimes be led me to dream: what could it look like to live in this broken world free of drama and tragic events? What about returning to an era where the screen did not dominate humankind's time? I felt caught in the endless loops of hustle culture, wrapped up in this digital age. I wanted to operate in the physical world around me, yet thought I wouldn't be able to get away from blue light or notifications. Then I met my now-fiancé, began getting to know his family, and learned it is possible — even today — to return to "simpler times." It is possible to slow down, to eliminate distractions and prioritize what matters to you. It is possible to be employed in physical labor yet not ignorant of what's going on in pop culture. It is possible to get dirt on your hands more often than you are on screens. To need a shower or muscle massage. To get cuts, scrapes, and bruises — little things that show you did something. It is possible to work hard for another's benefit and then fall into bed, physically drained and exhausted, but heart full. I used to think I was idealistic, that the lifestyle I longed for could only be found in a previous century, but now I know it's possible.

Like a Fairy Tale

This story captures the spring I got to know my now-fiancé. We were working in the church kitchen, cutting up strawberries the size of planets and fans. We were working in his parents' garden, forgetting to sprinkle Epsom salts (or the fairies' growing dust) on the roots of tomato plants. We were writing stories and poems. We were finding that the world is so much more than we thought it could be, and we got to share that magic with the other.

A Songbird's Summer

I didn't get to spend quite a few summers at home growing
up, but the one after I had found my niche was the hardest
of all. In accepting a "mutually beneficial scheme" from my
now-fiancé, I decided to undertake writing exercises that
would capture what I was observing throughout my
travels. I was trying to see the beauty I could not take in on
my own through the eyes of another. Having received the
last of my writing exercises, my now-fiancé was struck with
a story about a songbird who had to leave her home for the
winter. I absolutely loved the beginning he wrote, and
together we wielded words in an attempt to portray what a
songbird learned over a summer.

On the Road to Tomorrow

We all have darkness in our past — whether from shaping
influences or bad decisions — that often haunts us in the
present. Progressive sanctification is the journey of life, and
sometimes it can feel like you're taking two steps forward
and one step back. This process of trying to improve upon
the past, and all the demons that manifest from that, is a lot
of what my now-fiancé and I battled against the first fall we
shared. One of the nights during the month he was out of
the country, I was listening to "September 15, 2017: Cassini
- The Grand Finale" by Sleeping At Last and was struck
with an analogy for this part of our relationship. It had
been hard, but I wanted to capture that we were making
progress that was truly making a difference, and one day

we're going to make it to that heavenly shore—a reality we can't quite comprehend—and see that everything truly does have purpose.

Acknowledgments

The Neighborhood Kids: You filled my childhood with endless play. Thank you for the hours of Boy & Girl War, Nature Royalty, Town, and trekking all those paths I raked in the woods.

Heidi, Abbie, & Julia: My girls, with you the publication of stories took flight when we capped our eighth-grade year by forming B.A.A.T.H. (Baucom, Arnold, Alix, Thomas, Haase), the book club where we wrote instead of read. Although relatively unsuccessful and short-lived, I'm grateful for the experience and hope to have many more in the decades to come.

My Senior Life Group: You played a pivotal role in growing my relationship with Jesus. Thank you for how you love unconditionally, speak hard truth, and are so on-fire about your faith.

Caedmon Evans: You rewrote my story by merely being a friend. I am eternally grateful for how God worked through you to change me for good.

Kylie (Lewis) Norris: Thank you for the unexpected friendship we shared during my last semesters of college. You unintentionally showed me that lifestyles different from mine do not exclude another human being from the underlying themes we all share.

Ansa Katherine: You are my flashlight. From beating me up with a pillow for the original ending of "A Little Girl's Story" to your color-coated annotations, your feedback is rich in thought and insight. Thank you for keeping me real. Thank you for being excited for me.

Ella Grant & Nona Janowski: Thank you for your thoughts in giving feedback on these stories. Your perspectives continue to astound me. I am still simply surprised I get to be a beneficiary.

Nathan Janowski: Thank you for showing me these stories could be printed. I was about to let them fade into the past as a former hobby, but you wouldn't let me lose the dream a little girl once had. Thank you for not giving up on me.

Tech, Hospitality, & Facilities: For letting me step out of my positions to give these stories the time they needed. And every opportunity where we worked together before that. I had the best time serving with you.

Grace Trotter & Beth Snow: You jumped into these pages only weeks before they were printed. Thank you for the time you put into proofreading and giving feedback. We are better because of your efforts.

The Ross Janowski Girls: It is something different to see and hear the reactions you always imagined your audience having. Thank you for wanting to hear these stories, and for all the questions and comments that helped me refine them before publishing. I am continuously amazed by how each of you is mature beyond her years.